Let the Merry-Go-Round Resume

A Family Story

JOHN MURPHY

Let the Merry-Go-Round Resume
A Family Story

Vanguard Press

*Vanguard Press is an imprint of
Pegasus Elliot Mackenzie Publishers Ltd.*
www.pegasuspublishers.com

First Published in 2014

**Vanguard Press
Sheraton House Castle Park
Cambridge England**

Printed & Bound in Great Britain

Contents

1
Home

December 2012

Home is where the heart is they say. I'm not so sure, at the age of forty-five and back living with your mother it's not too exciting particularly when you don't get on, and because you resent the fact that although you own the place you can't actually do anything with it: sell it, move on, get the hell away from Stranraer that's the goal. But all that has changed overnight, my mother dead in December 2011, not a shock or should I say shouldn't have been a shock but actually is.

December 2010

I'd arrived back from Crosby, Liverpool, and I'd been working there in a *'living death'* style job: you turn up clock in you go and clock out. I'd been there six months and was finished. I'd been asked to stay another three months but didn't fancy another six months' lease on the flat. A one room bed-sit, complete with sink, microwave, TV, heater and bed which folded into the wall… communal toilet, shower and laundry services. In truth I'd been in worse but at my age I was certainly tiring of this

11

lifestyle. I tended to do IT contracts for six months for the public sector predominantly; go in, set something up and go. The money was okay but it was mind-numbing and six months here and six months there was taking its toll on my health... isolation. Solitude. Alcohol. There were times I wished I was a bricklayer-joiner or tradesman of some sort, a white van man. They seemed to have it sorted in my opinion, a social life, a family, friends (a life), down the pub on Friday night with the lads, night in with the woman on Saturday, day with the kids Sunday (simple).

I'd survived Xmas and New Year by never crossing the door. My mother was her usual annoying self, yapping about the family, which was effectively me (as my father was dead), but her obsession with her nephews and their wives and how perfect they were tended to always cause an argument.

My mothers' maiden name was Daltrey and if you had that name it was licence to do what you wanted:

- Strangle your wife
- General destruction
- Domestic violence
- Work optional (you're self-employed)
- Alcohol – You are not a drunk you are a character / *'an awfy man'*

In effect you could do no wrong... ever.

On the other hand if I held a lump of coal up and I said it was black she'd argue it was white. It seemed to be one rule for them (everyone else) and another for me. To give an example I'd been divorced for years now but she still wouldn't acknowledge it. I got on well with my ex-wife so we never had any problems and I spoke and saw her and my son on a regular basis. My mother of course blamed me for the divorce, I was a *'drunken whoremaster'* in her eyes, though I hadn't been doing that much *'whoremastering'* in a few years, so she just called me a drunkard (maternal praise indeed). I was convinced she had a personality disorder of some type, she seemed to have to blame someone for everything. She blamed me for everything, even making it rain. When I got divorced she ended up in the hospital with bowel problems. I actually thought she was going to die (so I was lead to believe anyway). At the time I was living in London, so it was a day's travel to get back. First words I got were, you guessed it.

"It's all **YOUR** bloody fault!"

After ten minutes of visiting her I left, there was nothing wrong with her gob. She'd been a musician in the past and I'm sure this had a lot to do with it. She was a 'show pony / drama queen', she craved attention and me being the only son I was the captive audience.

My father had been an alcoholic and tended to avoid her like the plague; latterly I could understand him, though in the past I'd had her effectively brainwashing me to side with her. When he died in 1996, I was glad he'd died before her. It wasn't that I wanted him dead but more to give her a break. It was, however, probably the worst thing that could have happened (for me anyway); she needed someone to chase after to yap, bully, seek attention from, generally moan at. I think the best description would be a '**Lightning Rod**'. When my father was younger he'd been a professional soldier for over a decade and I think he was

13

used to it (people shouting at you that is). I on the other hand was not. She liked to tell everyone about the life she'd had, about her life and family as a 'Professional Martyr'. What she sometimes forgot was that her martyr lifestyle seemed to affect everyone else around her and as an adult she had the ability to make choices.

Xmas Day had been a non-event, she'd been asked to go to one of my cousins, I think I got invited as an accessory so I was never that bothered. I'd been to a few before and just switched off, usually with the help of a heavy dose of drink. I had the obligatory argument with her before it and told her to "Fuck Off!" so I didn't bother going. The argument was about what time we were getting a lift at, and that was it, the reason to argue. At New Year I was expected to sit with her (the captive audience... but didn't) and bring in Hogmanay (a non-event if ever there was one). I sat up the stairs and watched a DVD and got drunk. Drink of course was banned from the house (at least for me) but she always seemed to produce it for herself. Yet again it was 'Do as I say! Not as I do!'

I heard her coming to bed screaming at my bedroom door then passing out whilst singing Danny Boy, not sure where that one came from it was certainly new to me. Anyway fuck knows?

February 2011

She'd been complaining about her ears continuously for over five years, and had been attending a doctor, though they just seemed to palm her off with creams, lotions etc.

I told her she was deaf. Of course though it was my fault for speaking softly. Never sure therefore why she couldn't ever hear the doorbell or TV?

Eventually they'd got an ENT Consultant to see her who decided he wanted a biopsy to see what was going on. I'd taken her down to Dumfries she stayed the night, and then got a nurse phoning me telling me she had cancer. So we picked her up (she demanded one of my cousins come with me) in hysterics.

Selfishly I was thinking of myself as she was prone to going mad at the slightest reason and according to her she'd been ill, dying, for years, but now she actually was.

Within two weeks of all this she was diagnosed with terminal cancer.

Primary Diagnosis: Ear Canal Cancer

To fix her she'd have needed all her right ear removed inner and outer, then radiotherapy and chemotherapy. After this her lower jaw would have had to go (as the cancer had spread), then they would have to rebuild the jaw and give her years of plastic surgery. So needless to say this was not an option for a woman who went into hysterics at the drop of a hat; she'd gone bonkers after a couple of MRI scans and I could hear her screaming her head off when she was in it. I was sure the panel of consultants were relieved when we left and declined any form of treatment, truth be told I doubt if I'd have bothered myself if I'd been in her shoes, it seemed brutal.

The trip home was an event, stuck in a car for three hours with my mother was bad enough, stuck in a car with my mother just being told she was completely fucked was an all-time great. Thankfully she was too shell-shocked to say anything.

March 2011 to December 2012

On hearing my mother was dying we had the usual response, loads of phone calls, the odd visits, flowers, tea and sympathy. The majority of this just passed me by, it took the deflection from me, so I made the most of it and kept my head down. I reckoned my mother would be dead by Xmas as I'd worked in the NHS for twenty years on and off so I knew the statistical probability of it all; the consultants agreed.

My mother at this stage was calling all the doctors in Stranraer a shower of cunts and incompetent bastards. So perhaps I was right after all, there was something wrong with her hearing. I knew acknowledgement of this fact however would never happen and the fact that I was correct would never register with her infallibility or 'Pope Syndrome'.

I put my job hunting on hold as I knew if I moved away for a job this would just result in crying and tantrums. I could imagine leaving, her then getting hospitalised and me having to come back anyway so I resigned myself to the fact that for at least the next six months I'd be dealing with a hysterical dying woman on my own. At least she hadn't blamed me for giving her cancer, so that was progress.

My personal regime seemed to consist of binges of fitness mixed with excessive bouts of alcohol. Anyway the months chuntered by, my ex-wife and son visited three times which was good, it broke the monotony something I'll always be grateful to them for. By the month of June she wouldn't leave the house, the cancer had affected her balance and she looked like a drunken sailor. We had a Macmillan Nurse visiting which was basically tea and sympathy, but it seemed to help her. Initially it was me that set up the visits, which irked her. "What do I want her coming here for!" I felt like replying, "My sanity".

Of course once they started attending it was as if it was all my mother's idea, though I didn't really care. She was on a concoction of painkillers that would floor an elephant, but added to that she was tippling on liquid morphine, so to say she was high would be the understatement of the year. She kept calling me Ted. That was my father's name and he'd been dead over a decade.

My ex-wife asked if coming the last week of October would be better than the following April, I told her my mother wouldn't make Xmas. I wasn't that keen on my ex-wife and son coming the last time. I could predict some sort of disaster ensuing, my mothers' hysterics were getting worse, though for once she actually had something to be hysterical about. I was more worried about my eight-year-old son, it wasn't something a child should see, at least in my opinion.

So as predicted my mother took a turn for the worse when they were both here and that dragged on for a few days. The following week after they had left I had her in a palliative care unit and she was dead within the month and that was really it. She didn't go well, a tumour impacting on the brain is not a pleasant way to go.

After the death the usual recriminations with the relations. They of course had been arguing that she didn't need to be in the hospital but should be at home. I told them she could fuck'n move in with them. Then it was move her into a flat, then a care home. Of course they got social services involved who I told to "Fuck off". They wanted the bed and I said no, but it didn't matter she was dead in days. So it seemed I was right (for once again, habit forming). Dead within four weeks of being admitted, it all seemed so sudden. I thought I would have been ready. One of my cousin's wife had arrived to tell me as I had the phone off the hook as I was sick of the hospital phoning in the middle of the night and then marching up to the hospital for them to tell me they'd knocked her out with morphine. My cousin's wife arrived with a young cop in tow, I hadn't spoken to any of them since she went to hospital. Well I did tell them to all go and fuck themselves so it had been a pretty one-sided conversation. I don't know how they thought I'd react. I ended up throwing up quite violently. Anyway that was the end or the beginning of the end as they say.

The Funeral

So the funeral arrangements were made, pretty easily actually. Stranraer was a one-horse town, so there was a limited amount of funeral directors and the guy that ran it I'd been to school with. It seemed to be more of a reunion than arranging the funeral. I wanted a private ceremony; of course the relations wanted a state funeral akin to Comrade Stalin. So yet another disagreement, the repercussions were now starting to set in. I wasn't particularly talking (or wanting to talk) to anyone. Anyway I'd made the arrangements the way I fuck'n wanted. I couldn't get a lot of things out of my mind. The last time I saw her was on the Monday and she was dead on the Thursday. I had visited her periodically over her time in hospital.

The day after I put her in I went to visit her and she was sitting wanting to come home. I said "No" and that seemed to be the end of that visit. The relations of course were telling me that she had to come home, I told them she could move in with them if they were so keen for her to come out. Then it was we'll get her a flat, move into a home blah fuck'n blah.

I think what they failed to grasp was that she was finished and had weeks to live. The last straw I had with the relations (or so I thought) was with them contacting social services and some dumb-ass social worker telling me they'd be moving her out into a home as she had a one- to six-month life expectancy. She was dead within three days.

So the funeral came and went: a private ceremony, tense. Of course I got drunk before, during and after. Thank fuck it was all over in an hour. Called a few of the relations 'pikeys' and that was it.

A few weeks after her death my blood pressure went through the roof as I read my mother's obituary in the local rag. No mention of myself, scant mention of my father, just a let's fly the 'Daltrey Flag' high. Let's mention the lot of them, even the ones that have been dead for years. Funny. I'd been the one looking after her for the previous year, hauling her out of bed, hauling her off the toilet, doing all the domestics, but who the fuck did I think I was, I was just her simple son.

I responded with a letter to the local paper telling them what the fuck did they think they were playing at, also slagging the relations to the core. It didn't get printed. I wrote another letter telling the editor of the paper if I'd written a letter about dog shite on the pavement would he have printed it.

He phoned me to tell me that he'd print my original letter and that's where we are.

So I'm waiting for things such as the will to be processed, another case of my mother fucking up as the solicitor she used I didn't find that entertaining with costs so I've had to transfer to another solicitor.

So waiting, just waiting for what I don't know, perhaps inspiration.

2

The Beginning

It was another world when my mother Audrey was born it was
17th September 1930 somewhere in rural Galloway. She had a
brother (Jimmie) John who had been born the previous year, my
mother had been a sickly child but it was basically down to
poverty. Her father was a blacksmith, her mother worked the
land in essence a rural existence, living in a cottage, with some
extra tenant land. My grandmother had come from quite a well
to do family but had married a man of dubious temperament, as
her sister liked to remind her. Her sister had married a local
businessman: he owned a garage. My grandfather had descended
from Irish travellers – tinkers – but had decided to put down
roots in Scotland. He had had a strange upbringing in that he had
been brought up a Protestant but his sister had been brought up
a Roman Catholic, the result of what was deemed in those days
a 'mixed marriage'. His sister Kate had married an Englishman
who did a 'collar and tie' job for the post office. They had a son
James. The religion resulted in a lot of grief locally, every man
and his dog was a member of the 'Masonic Lodge' apart from
Dermot. He also had a habit of singing Irish songs in the pub
which didn't go down well locally and usually ended up in an
argument, physical or verbal.

Audrey's father (Dermot) had followed in his father's footsteps in that he was a violent alcoholic. His own father had died in a mental institution for the criminally insane; he had tried to strangle his wife to death in a drunken rage. There were numerous occasions of domestic violence and general lunacy, the smashing of furniture, sometimes the smashing of bones.

Audrey's father beat her brother and mother on numerous occasions over the years, usually in a drunken rage or worse, when suffering a weeklong hangover. Her father had been a champion boxer in his day and had worked on occasion as a boxer when the Irish travellers came round once a year operating fairgrounds. If you could last three rounds with him you got paid. They didn't pay out too often. Someone battering metal all day in front of a raging furnace can usually be deemed to be quite 'hard'.

The cottage was fairly simple consisting of three rooms and a bathroom: two bedrooms, living room and kitchen and bathroom. A coal fire was always raging in the main room. Out the back there was some land that was rented, some owned, keeping an assortment of animals, and also staple foods grown such as potatoes. The main income generator was money that came in from Dermot's work as a blacksmith and musician. There was a smithy attached to the cottage, basically what you need is a large raging furnace and the tools and skills, passed from generation. My grandfather Dermot had been a champion blacksmith and had won numerous 'Agricultural Shows' and in his later life had went on to judge these competitions. He also ran his own band and was a fine button box accordion player. The band played traditional Scottish music and were in high demand for local rural dances, weddings etc. I always thought it ironic that someone who could bring such pleasure with his hands could bring such abject misery.

My grandfather had that true Dr Jekyll and Mr Hyde quality in that everyone thought what great guy he was until the doors closed at home and perhaps then his true dark side appeared.

July 1935

It was a warm summer's night in the village of Glenluce in Galloway. Dermot Daltrey had just left one of the local pubs, the 'Horse & Cart'. He was a big man, six foot two and built to match. He had that afternoon been playing football for his local team 'Galloway Hibernian'. He played in goal. Basically, score against him and you were dead. He had quite a lot of 'clean sheets' funnily enough. The drinking had started before the match, during it (at least half-time) and after it. Drinking in Scotland is usually to excess even in these days. It was now roughly one a.m. – so much for Dermot getting up in the morning to milk the couple of cows he kept, but that was Elizabeth's job. After all she only had two toddlers to bring up. Cows need milking on a regular basis or they tend to literally explode. He jumped in his ramshackle van and drove the four miles back to the cottage. Nobody was bothered with drink driving in those days. Dermot was all over the road, cursing and ranting the result of the match a lifetime ago, now raging that he had spent so much money, losing at cards in a back room and getting totally drunk, it was a miracle he had never crashed one of these days coming back on this all too familiar journey. He had the eyesight of a bat and wore 'milk bottle specs' to match. He swerved continuously, going up the embankment more than once.

He finally arrived crashing the van into a wheelbarrow in front of the house, he'd run over a few cats and dogs in his time that was for sure, unable to find his key kicking at the door screaming to be let in:

"Open the fuck'n door, ya fuck'n bitch! Open the fuck'n door, or I'll kill the lot of you'se."

Elizabeth finally let him in. She was exhausted. She'd been looking after the children, the beasts, the cooking and cleaning, she knew she'd have to get up at dawn for the milking and it was now just after one a.m., the fun and games had just started.

"Whaur's ma dinner, whaur the fuck is ma dinner, ya lazy bitch! C'mon hurry up."

Elizabeth went to the stove, one of those old fashioned ones run by the coal fire, a couple of old blackened pots sitting on top, one filled with potatoes the other with minced beef, one of the staple diets to this day in Scotland: 'mince and tatties'.

Dermot sat at the kitchen table shouting abuse. Elizabeth going as fast as she could, he cursed and ranted, telling her how fuck'n useless she was, how pathetic, what a fuck'n whore she was, how she had driven his family away from him, how she had dragged him down, what a weight she was around his neck, how he could have done oh so much better, how he'd be such better off without her.

Audrey and Jimmie lay in their beds cowering, knowing what would be coming later, not knowing that in later life this would be coming to them, this was their future a mirror reflection, the endless nights that would be like this, the never ending nights, the screaming, the shouting, the violence.

Dermot gorged himself on the food, demanding more, but there was no more. Elizabeth felt a backhander to her face. It was her fault. He was a working man, he needed proper food, not this pig swill. She went flying across the room, she was just over five feet in height, her mouth bleeding, silent tears as this was her fate, thinking only of Audrey and Jimmie. Now his attention was solely on her, he slapped her again, grabbing her nightie with one hand, slapping her with the other, blood streaming from her mouth.

He was not shouting anymore just talking with venom, rage in his eyes holding her down over the table, telling her how he could easily kill her, how he could snap her like a twig, telling her what a whore she was, how he hated her. He looked at the accordion sitting in the corner of the room, however he hadn't music on his mind.

He undid the belt on his trousers, unbuttoned his trousers. He held her down with his left hand wrapping it round her throat tightly squeezing the life out of her, his right hand went up under her nightie. He pulled her drawers down then forced himself into her. He was in a drunken state. He pumped and pounded furiously, panting like a crazed dog. He was getting nowhere, no release. He pulled himself out manhandled her so she was face down on her stomach on the table. He forced himself inside her, this time though sodomising her, slapping the back of her head sporadically, forcing himself on her as hard as possible. He panted wildly. Elizabeth's release was tears, they were not of joy.

Dermot pulled himself out staggered to the chair beside the fire, his chair, his domestic throne. He was the master of the house.

Elizabeth staggered to the bedroom. Checking on the children, both of them pretending to be asleep, she went to her bedroom. It was now after three a.m. She'd be up in a few hours, for the milking. Even the beasts had time to rest. She never had time to rest she just had to get on with it she'd made her bed now she had to lie in it. She knew when she got up he'd still be in the chair, still half drunk, now hung-over. Hopefully by the time she got back from the milking and feeding he'd be gone, more likely sleeping it off in bed, going off for the next round of drinking. The drinking stopped when the money ran out or physically he could take no more. His body said no not his mind.

Elizabeth cried uncontrollably. This time there were no silent tears. Audrey and Jimmie lay listening, Audrey crying, Jimmie pretending he was sleeping.

At five a.m. Elizabeth got up aching. She was exhausted. She was thirty years of age but she looked in her late forties, a lifetime of hard labour, sleepless nights had aged her quickly in the last decade after her marriage to Dermot. At first the marriage had been fine, but her family were not at all impressed. He was a no-user in their eyes, not from good stock, no prospects, no use. Dermot's parents were much the same, at least his mother was, there was no real sense coming from his father. Dermot was thirty-seven, considerably older, both his parents now dead, both dying in their fifties, one dying in an institution. Dermot had avoided the 'Great War' as he was working the land, but he was technically Irish too.

Elizabeth walked the short walk to the byre, getting the feed for the six cows they owned, walking to the field and shouting

"Hay up! Hay up!"

This was to attract the cows who were there waiting already, waiting to be fed, waiting for water to be put into the water tank. She fed the chickens she kept, checking the coop for eggs, putting them in a basket. Four chickens, three eggs, and a nasty big rooster.

She thought of how life could have been if she'd taken a different path. She'd had suitors when she was young, all of whom had gone on to marry other girls, all of whom seemed to have easier lives, who seemed to have some sort of happiness in their life. She didn't have a life she just existed. Just like the beasts she was feeding she was just a beast of burden.

Elizabeth led the cows into the barn. She sat on the milking stool, got a bucket and went to work, it was now six thirty a.m. She put the milk into urns. These would be picked up by the man from the milk company.

She went back to the cottage. Dermot had disappeared from the chair. He had moved himself to the bedroom and was flat out with his clothes on.

Elizabeth washed herself in the kitchen sink. She looked in a mirror, her face had bruises and her lip was split, looking at her future. At the age of thirty she had a full set of false teeth, it seemed to be the way back then. She threw some pieces of wood and coals on to the fire, sat in the chair and dozed, she'd get perhaps an hour of sleep if she was lucky. The children wouldn't show till around eight a.m. if she was lucky.

She thought of her childhood. It had been fairly privileged, she'd wanted for nothing, clothes, food, and her parents had been kind and loving. Both of them religious, both of them tee-total, quite a contrast to what she was now experiencing in matrimonial bliss. She'd had an older brother but he had come down with fever and died when he was twelve years old. She had been nine years old. She also had a surviving sister who lived locally. She had pleasant memories of playing in the summer in the woods, climbing trees, playing football. Her parents had only recently died, two years ago. She missed them terribly. At least she had inherited a little money, this had helped ride the tide when Dermot had gone on bouts of the drink. Dermot was lucky as he was the only local blacksmith, reliable when sober, not so reliable when otherwise indisposed, so the work was always there.

She awoke to hear the milk truck, the milkman taking the urns and leaving empty ones, she dozed off again. Jimmie appeared and awoke her. He played with a wooden truck on the table, she got him some bread and jam and made herself some tea. Dermot appeared, no acknowledgement of what had happened the night before, but that was hardly unusual. He grunted like an animal, just wanting fed. She cooked him some of the eggs in a frying pan, gave it to him with some bread and tea. He drank it black with sugar. He'd changed out of his clothes of the night before into work clothes with tackety boots to match. He went to the sink and washed himself then grunted that he was going to shoe some horse, and off he went.

They heard him go to the smithy, pick up some readymade horseshoes and tools, then heard the van doors close, the engine start, the wheels creaking down the road till silence. Audrey appeared. She helped herself to the bread and jam and the pot of tea.

Elizabeth went to lie down, she could deal with the cleaning later. The cows would need milking later on in the day, who knows what time Dermot would arrive back, or in what state. It was like a merry go round, except you could get off of a merry go round, but not this one this was for eternity, this was for keeps.

Dermot drove the van down the country lane. He had one job on for the day. It was a farmer called MacIntosh. He resented the farmers, he knew they looked down at him. He was a peasant in their eyes. He hated the fact that they had been born into wealth, born into privilege. Dermot though could read and write and count, in his eyes that was all the education you needed to get by on in life.

He drove up to the farmhouse. The job was a fairly big one; he had to shoe a team of Clydesdale horses. People tended to think that dealing with the Clydesdales was dangerous and hard. It was hard but the Clydesdales were docile and never any problem to deal with.

He went round the horses one by one, removing the old shoes and cleaning out the hoofs before putting on the ready-made shoes. It was a morning's work and a back breaking experience. The farmer left him to it and this suited him fine. He knew what the response from the farmer would be when he asked for payment:

"Yeh'll have to wait till the end of the month."

He cleaned up, went to the farm with a receipt he'd written up handing it to MacIntosh, barely acknowledging the farmer's existence and walked back to the van. He started the van and steered it round and drove down the lane, looking into the farmers' fields filled with dairy cattle. This was what made the money in the area, agriculture. There were sheep farms in the hills, dairy cattle in the lower fields. Some farmers had arable and grew various crops. The land round here was fairly blessed, plenty of rainfall and with the Gulf Stream hitting the local coast the weather was never that extreme.

Dermot had a thirst now and he knew how to quench it. He drove a few miles to the local village, back to the same pub he'd been in the night before, probably the same faces sitting in the same seats, telling the same stories, drinking being the sole purpose.

He thought of Elizabeth. He had pangs of guilt of his behaviour, but not many, it would pass. His crocodile tears were short-lived; he rarely thought of the children but did so now, thinking of his own childhood, his father the same as him. Maybe it was his destiny; the apple doesn't fall far from the tree. He had loved his mother and sister, his sister Kate had married that well-to-do Englishman Ken. She had a teenage son, James, and seemed happy. Her own house, her husband a manager in the post office. They sometimes came to visit, had done so last year, staying in the local hotel this time, his sister always siding with him, never disagreeing, always supporting him. It was never his fault, he could do no wrong in her eyes. She was always on at him to convert religions, a sore point for her.

an aircraft went overhead. Sometimes he lost control of his mind, taking hours to come back to reality, the children cruelly laughing unaware of the images ravaging inside the man's head. Jimmie was shouting every time an aircraft went overhead:

"Plane, sir!"

"Germans, sir!"

The school was located on a hill overlooking Luce Bay which was part of the Irish Sea, so Jimmie had taken to shouting: "Periscope, sir!", "Submarines, sir!", and "Germans, sir!", the result being everyone scuttling out to the trench no matter what the weather, the teacher phoning the local police station, the police becoming aware of this sad situation, the police not knowing how to react.

The whole point of the children's education was basically to let them have the ability to read and write and do basic arithmetic, enough to get them by on for the rest of their lives. Their lives had been chartered out already. They'd more than likely follow their parents' footsteps. All of them were already working the land. Jimmie was learning his father's trade but also helping out when the time came round for things like 'tattie hoking', helping Elizabeth with the animals, doing a lot of the jobs she used to do on her own, lightening her burden. Audrey was a weak child, waif-like, bothered with her lungs, unable to do any hard work, but no one bothered, they all loved her.

One of the boys at school had pushed her over, the teacher had gone berserk belting the boy senseless with a thick leather tawse, before Jimmie meted out his own brand of justice. Dermot was teaching Jimmie boxing, though Dermot more than often got carried away, forgetting he was hitting a child. The teacher liked Audrey. In his eyes she had talent. She knew music, so she was one up on the majority of the children, she was different.

The school teacher liked Dermot until he accused Jimmie of stealing this was something Dermot could not abide. Dermot visited the teacher and read him the riot act. After that, the teacher was very wary of one Mr Dermot Daltrey. Jimmie then felt the full force of Dermot. Whether he had ever stolen the teacher's shovel, no one ever found out. Jimmie was saying nothing.

1942

By 1942 the War had been going for the best part of two to three years but it was what they called the 'phoney war'. Bombers hit Britain, bombers hit Germany, the Atlantic Convoys suffered. The war in North Africa raged, the War in the Far East had started. All of this seemed like a world away. It was a rural existence. With the exception of rationing and seeing the POWs sometimes marching around, sometimes troops on manoeuvre particularly at the coast looking for agents being dropped there was no way you could tell a war was going on.

A lot of the young men had been drafted, some exempt as they were in protected occupations, war girls brought in to work the land as well. There had also been a limited influx of children from the cities, the cities the ones being bombed by the Luftwaffe. The influx was small and nowhere near as big as in England. As Dermot would say when drunk, *'there'll always be an England as Scotland stands',* it was a take on a wartime song.

Everyone hating the rationing, but in the countryside food could be easily obtained: rabbits, go to the shore and do some fishing. The adults hated tobacco rationing, the children sweets rationing, but in the countryside it could be plentiful. Dermot had contacts who would take things off his hands. Thieving was a crime, poaching, however, was a way of life.

Jimmie was thirteen years of age, Audrey was twelve years old. Jimmie had started learning the blacksmith trade following in the foot-steps of his father, in more ways than one. It was the way. School finished at fourteen years old and you went out and worked – no welfare state. Audrey learned the piano and the accordion, Dermot took great interest in this, he was more interested in her doing this than wasting her time on school books and such. Jimmie got to go out and play with the other kids at night, gathering in the local fields, playing football with the other boys, catching rabbits with bag nets, going fishing to the local burns whilst Audrey practised.

Elizabeth soldiered on, haggard beyond her years, but Jimmie could help out with the beasts, Audrey in the house. She'd taken to smoking, at first not letting Dermot know, scared of the inevitable reaction, another wrong on her behalf, something else he could beat her with, complain about the cost. She sometimes took some of his whisky when he was out. It eased her pain. Dermot's drinking getting worse, his temper more and more out of control, the beatings harder, Jimmie sometimes taking the brunt of these, attending school black and blue, no one saying a thing, some other children suffering the same fate, the teacher turning a blind eye. No such thing as social services. He fell, should be more careful.

The house had had an extension built on, another bedroom, Dermot and Audrey now separated; more privacy for both of them in their teenage years, better for Jimmie as he could sneak in and out at all hours, Audrey more privacy to practice her music.

Dermot's band was still in full swing but now they had a star attraction, a child prodigy. To Audrey this was a different world but tiring. Sometimes she wouldn't be back till three or four a.m. and if Dermot had brought some of his cronies back to the house, the party was just starting. She was the canary expected to entertain. This had happened on numerous occasions even when the band were not playing, Audrey hauled out of bed to entertain, 'no' not an option.

Jimmie was jealous of Audrey's new-found fame, her picture in the local papers 'The Wonder Accordionist', 'The Musical Prodigy'. She'd even gotten to play on national radio. She had entered a world he could only dream of. He'd started playing practical jokes on her, though one had back fired when he'd dropped a slab of rock on her bare foot, removing one of her toes. He was mortified. Dermot punished him severely, who knows what the outcome if it had been a finger.

Elizabeth was glad Audrey had learnt the music; it would stand her in good stead. She led a lonely existence, her older sister occasionally visited with her family, but only when she knew Dermot wouldn't be there, usually when he was off to one of his 'Agricultural Shows'. Her sister was four years older than Elizabeth but looked ten years younger. Elizabeth had become waif-like and nervous, jumping out of her skin at the slightest noise, her sister putting a brave face on it, lying to her, telling her how well she looked, both of them knowing this was a lie. Elizabeth was always struggling for money, Dermot controlling the purse strings giving her house-keeping, never enough though. Funnily though he always made sure the children were well clothed. Appearances were important to Dermot.

The band was in big demand though in no small thanks to Audrey. She had become a local attraction and Dermot was getting bookings all over. Sometimes they'd go away and stay the night at B&B's in different places; there were local bookings, but sometimes functions such as weddings, birthdays, ceilidhs. The band was hot stuff. Within the band there was Dermot and Audrey, another accordionist Kathy, a drummer Neil and two fiddlers, John and Jimmie. The core of the band though, was Dermot and Audrey. It was Dermot's band and everyone knew it.

Audrey loved the mayhem at these events particularly the big functions in the local town halls though she hated standing up on the stage. She suffered from panic attacks, but Dermot wasn't the type to take no for an answer, there was no stage fright allowed here. Stage Fright would have to deal with Dermot's fists.

When Audrey looked down from the stage all she could see were lots of young men and women dancing together, having a good time, dancing, drinking, smoking, laughing, smoking and she was the cause. She liked looking at the men all dressed up, some in uniform. The place was filled with smoke and the smell of stale drink. She liked looking at the style of the women, the clothes they wore the make-up, you would never had thought there was a war on.

The men all out looking for romance or maybe just sex, some of them back on leave, some of them waiting to be drafted, some of them in the process of training. A lot of them drowning their sorrows, drinking for today, dancing for today, living for today, make the most of what you have when you have it. The woman all out looking for men: get themselves a man, you don't want to be last left on the shelf, that wouldn't do, what would people think.

Audrey, although young, was quite mature for her age. She wasn't dressed as a schoolgirl she was dressed as a young woman, sex sells. Unfortunately some young men had reciprocated her smiles, much to Dermot's fury, Audrey getting hard icy stares from Dermot the lads in question being taken behind the hall at the interval and beaten relentlessly. Dermot coming back his white shirt splattered in blood, though not his. Audrey, nervous of his rages, she had only ever suffered the verbal ones.

The War the main topic of conversation, rumours abounding, German agents everywhere, fifth columnists everywhere, traitors everywhere. What was Davie MacDonald doing on the hill looking on to the bay in the middle of the night with a flashlight? What was Sheila Agnew doing on her own walking along the beach at all hours, her a married woman as well.Sometimes near the end, the drink taking effect on a lot of the men resulting in fighting, long held grudges between families going back generations, cliques and clans. You fall out with one and you fall out with the lot of them, no one backing down. Sometimes razor blades getting used, things getting out of control. The local 'Bobbie' always hanging around at the hall, truncheon in hand, justice meted out severely to anyone getting too carried away, sometimes the local minister there, 'fights okay, fornication no'. When these events finished everyone ended up staggering out, the majority walking home as fuel was on ration. Drink was supposed to be on ration too, but in the hills there were lots of local brews and stills, if you didn't care too much for your eyesight.

Dermot's drinking had grown to excess, his blacksmithing days were getting less and less. He was making more money from the band. He also preferred the lifestyle, all day in bed, all night out playing. Music and drinking. Usually by the end of the night Dermot these days was just poured into a car, and driven home. When he got back home he usually crashed out in the chair in front of the fire, or went straight to bed with Elizabeth. He hated Elizabeth. She was in his way, he could have been a player, she was holding him back, the band could travel all over, they could go all the way, Elizabeth was in the way.

He'd come home with Audrey and packed her off to bed. He lay with Elizabeth, dreaming of what could have been, in his eyes what should be.

Awake – 1943

The band were doing well, bookings were coming in, the money was flowing, everyone was happy, what more could they all want? Dermot could afford to do what he wanted, all he was doing was training Jimmie to follow in his shoes. If only he'd been musical too, things would be easy; a moving fluent band, no blacksmithing, easy work.

It was a venue like any other, just the usual, a Masonic hall, the masons everywhere. Dermot hated the Masons, he never knew whether he was Protestant or Catholic. He was a mongrel. In rural Scotland the Masons ruled, all the bars and halls had their influence so he had to kowtow but he knew how to play them, making Audrey a member of the 'Eastern Star' then they'd be happy. Everyone was raising money for the war effort, perhaps some more than others, perhaps some of them caring more than others, profits more profitable than for the boys in uniform.

They'd arrived early to the venue in Kirkcolm. It was the usual gig the usual venue, it all had to be done one way or the other. Dermot let the rest of the band set up the instruments. There'd be no practice here, they could play the stuff they'd be doing here backwards. It was nothing complex, just the usual.

Dermot had a bottle in his coat pocket. He wandered off into the early cool night air. It was September around, six p.m. a mild night, still daylight. He smoked furiously on a roll-up. He looked around, no one watching, got his half-bottle from his coat pocket and quenched his thirst. He'd needed that. He kept slugging and felt better for it, paranoia now hitting him, it was his band he could do what he wanted, fuck the lot of them.

He threw the empty into the woods and went back, his thick specs covering up the fact that his eyes were gone, no one knowing if he was drunk or sober or hopefully somewhere in between. If he was sober he was angry and miserable, if he was drunk he was angry and angrier. Better to get him somewhere in between then life seemed to be easier for everyone.

The instruments were all set up. The days before anything electric. It was relatively simple. Dermot headed for the bar,

Audrey was sitting on the stage her legs dangling off of it, drinking lemonade and eating a sandwich. He looked at her with loathing, she was spoilt rotten, the amount of money he'd spent on her, too many young men looking at her as well. He drained a double whisky at the bar. Neil the drummer said,

"You're hitting it hard tonight, Dermot. Yeh okay?"

Dermot just gave him a look, it was enough. Neil had seen those looks before and what usually followed after them. The rage was about to hit and as long as it didn't hit him so be it.

The gig went off without major incident, a few scuffles but nothing serious. One half of the hall male, the other female the homemade bar doing a roaring trade, a mix of servicemen on leave and farm workers and locals, everything supposed to be on ration but for the night everything taken to excess. The boys plucking up more courage to approach the girls, the old Scottish dance band favourites played with speed. Near the end of the night the place like a furnace, everyone sweating everyone in a trance not wanting the night to end. Some boys picking up girls probably heading for the local woods looking for sex, not always romance, drunken fumbling, drunken kissing, drunken sex. Young girls wanting to feel grown-up to feel like women, some already more experienced beyond their years.

Dermot staring at Audrey with a loathing and rage for her, an overwhelming feeling of jealousy, she was the centre of attraction. In effect he was starting to feel surplus to requirements but it was his band and no one had better forget it.

He got his cut from the ticket sales and bar and divided it between the band members, though none for Audrey, also helping himself to a bottle of whisky and a couple of packs of

43

fags as well that would do for a nightcap. One of the unofficial perks.

The band packed up their stuff and went their separate ways. Kathy, the other piano accordionist, got a lift with Dermot and Audrey, the two females half sleeping on the way back a journey of about fifteen miles. Kathy was dropped off in town, little chance of being stopped by the police for drink driving in those days though road blocks were used by the military when they were around.

Dermot unpacked the accordions, his little button-box accordion compared to Audrey's large piano accordion. He was in one of his moods, ranting and raving, cursing and swearing, bringing up all the events of the past. His side of the story at least, believe it if you want, perhaps the rewriting of history in a lot of cases. How he'd been discriminated against, how everyone hated him, why should he care, what a useless wife he had. The verbal abuse had just started, the more whisky he poured down the more abusive he became, starting to threaten the household with violence. He went to his and Elizabeth's bedroom, slamming the door, Audrey and young Dermot listening to the ranting and raving of a madman then the screaming of their mother, not wanting to listen to this but feeling compelled to. Why was he such a bastard? Both of the children wanting it to end. Once the blows had started it usually ended in crying and screaming from Elizabeth to stop and just a torrent of abuse from Dermot. Then he'd restart the physical abuse and retreat to the kitchen. He had once lined up all the kitchen knives on the table and told them all to take their pick. He said he knew they all wanted him dead. He'd then staggered off and slept in the woods.

Dermot slammed the bedroom door falling into the chair shouting why the fire was dying out, he was forced to throw some wood and shovel some coal on to the fire, a major hassle for him. At least she'd had the sense to leave some sandwiches out for him. He ate the sandwiches, dropping half of it on the floor, still managing to scream and shout abuse, mainly about her deficiencies and that of her family, why they all hated him and his sister, how they all wanted him dead. He dozed in the seat for about half an hour. It was three thirty a.m. now, he needed entertained in other ways, ways he'd recently been thinking of, Elizabeth not in her prime in his eyes.

He opened Audrey's door and closed it quietly. She was sleeping, the house now quiet, but the animal was awake. He dropped his trousers and pants, not fully taking them off, still with his shoes on. All he had on top was a sweaty shirt and waistcoat. He pulled the blankets off Audrey, placing his left hand over her mouth, telling her to be quiet and how much he loved her.

All Audrey had on was panties and a nightie. The panties were pulled down roughly. He slid his fingers inside her, Audrey was more in shock than fear. He took his left hand from her mouth and drunkenly kissed her. All she could taste and smell was his sweat and the reek of strong booze. She was still in shock; this wasn't supposed to happen. He then got on top of her, grabbing both her bum cheeks, left hand to left cheek and vice versa. He entered her roughly, her tiny body taking his weight.

He started slowly telling her to keep quiet and how special she was, how she was his favourite. He then started fucking her roughly. Losing control he groaned as he pumped his sperm inside her. He pulled himself of her and pulled up his pants and trousers, making himself look presentable, Audrey pulling her panties up and pulling the blankets back up as far as she could, looking for a shield of protection, still in shock of what had happened. He left the bedroom saying nothing.

Audrey lay awake. She was still stunned as to what had happened. She heard Dermot collapse into the chair by the fire. Every once in a while he'd mumble to himself. Audrey eventually drifted off into a deep sleep. She awoke thinking had it all been a dream? Had she thought it all up?

She eventually got up, everyone letting her sleep as she'd had a late night, her mother with a swollen lip and bruised face hobbling around the main room like a crippled maid. Dermot had disappeared off to do a job, or not as the case may be. Maybe work, maybe mischief.

Jimmie as was outside talking to a couple of German POWs. Jimmie now liked them. They made him laugh and always brought him some sort of toy they'd made. Jimmie always acquired some eggs for the Germans. He had come to like them, their accents and the fact they would play football with him. These were the nation of toymakers who had started a world war.

End of 1943–44

By the end of 1943, Kate's son in Derby, James, was flying with the RAF in Bomber Command. He was a wireless operator in a crew flying a Halifax bomber. When Dermot had heard he went berserk telling his sister what a fool the boy was, how he'd be killed.

Audrey looked at the photos of James. He looked so smart. He had reached the rank of Flight Sergeant. He had come up to visit in the summer of 1943 with Kate, him in his uniform. He'd been on active service for over a year now. He never really talked about what he was doing, used to tell Jimmie it was all top secret. When he left it would be the last time they'd ever see him again. They took him and Kate to the local train station and said their goodbyes, Dermot telling them both to look after themselves, lecturing James about what was he thinking of joining the RAF, the stress it was having on his mother every time she turned on the radio with losses being announced all the time, it was goodbye then forever.

The abuse of Audrey continued. It had been going on for months. Foreplay seemed to consist for Dermot of beating up his wife in a drunken stupor and then having sex with his daughter. His sexual demands becoming more depraved and extreme as time went on. It was obvious to Elizabeth and Jimmie what was going on but there was nothing they could do, just accept it, there was a war going on.

Things came to a head though when Audrey started having miscarriages on a continuous basis, the local doctor not quite sure how to proceed or what was going on. Audrey clammed up, not engaging with other children her age, just spending a lot of time on her own, withdrawn.

The notification of James's death came at the end of December 1944. He had been missing in action for months, the terrible news inevitable.

Derby, Jan 1945

Elizabeth used the death of James as an excuse to send Audrey away to Derby. Audrey had become thin and gaunt, wrapped up in her world of abuse. She had told Dermot his sister needed the company. Dermot more interested in his own personal situation: loss of ticket sales, loss of his warped personal pleasures. He did however say nothing.

Audrey was packed off on the train, a long journey for a young girl with several changes. It was a big outing for her. She hadn't even commented on whether she wanted to stay or go. Dermot had said nothing when she left, just simmering in his own selfish thoughts; Elizabeth would more than likely pay tonight for her troubles.

Audrey had gotten a window seat. She liked travelling on the train watching the world pass her by. She looked at the countryside, the snow on the hills. She saw horses, sheep, goats, cows. She also liked coming into the big towns. She had never really visited a big city apart from Glasgow on a number of occasions with her mother, buying clothes and other things you couldn't get in a rural area. The hustle and bustle of the big towns and cities excited her. It was all a great adventure.

She had to change at Crewe to get a connection to Derby. The station was packed; servicemen and servicewomen coming home, going to bases, even some Americans, a couple of black men. She'd never seen a black person before. How strange.

This was the first time she'd been to Derby. She couldn't remember ever meeting Kate's husband before. His name was Kenneth, her Uncle Ken then. Kate met her off the train and took her down an old cobbled street. She looked around, loads of cobbled streets winding around.

Kate took her to a local café and bought her some cake and a pot of tea. Kate babbled away, Audrey was just nodding. Audrey was wondering how Kate really felt. She'd been close to her son; he had written to her all the time, telling her of his RAF training, never though telling her of the dangers, telling her of all the friends he'd made not the ones lost. The last time Audrey had seen him he seemed like the world was on his shoulders. Perhaps he knew he wouldn't survive the war. Audrey had had a childhood crush on him; she missed him too.

Kate took her to her home. It was a small attached house with two bedrooms, living room, indoor toilet and bathroom and kitchen. Audrey would be in James's room.

It was the first time she'd met Uncle Ken. He gave her a hug and kissed her on the cheek. He smelt of tobacco. He was a pipe smoker; she could see an array of pipes on the mantelpiece above the coal fire. He asked her questions on what was happening at home. She'd answered the majority of questions on walking back to the house with Kate. Kate was getting the dinner ready. Her mother Elizabeth had sent her away with a couple of pounds of cheese and a couple of pounds of bacon, worth its weight in gold everything being rationed, a roaring black-market in the towns.

The dinner was ready, a small table laid, pork sausages and mashed potatoes. Audrey felt relaxed here. They both pampered and spoiled her. There was apple crumble and custard, it was the first time Audrey had cleaned her plate. She had lost a lot of weight but she was built like a rake before so she looked haggard and gaunt. The difference here was she felt relaxed, she felt safe.

They listened to the radio broadcasts, intently upsetting when the casualties came in, the grief coming back, the memories, the lost love.

Audrey went to James's bedroom it didn't look like they'd changed anything, as if they expected him to walk through the door: pictures, photographs, model airplanes a small pocket sized RAF bible. She unpacked. The room had been cleaned recently, she could smell the polish, the wardrobe had been cleared. She only had the one suitcase, just arrived with the bare necessities as this was all she had anyways.

She looked through his stuff. Just young boys toys, penknife, football pennants and old tickets, comics, magazines and a few books. She laughed when she saw the Biggles front cover. She got ready and jumped in, Kate came up and said goodnight. She drifted off quickly she felt safe for the first time in a long time.

The routine was familiar. The same every day. They didn't bother with schooling, she was only here for a short period, she could leave school this year anyway. She helped Kate round the house but used to see some local girls who lived in the same street. One of them had an old piano which Audrey sometimes played, the other neighbours would sometimes come round and it could end up in a late night but all very tame in comparison to what she was used to seeing. Not much Scottish music here: more wartime favourites, the sort of stuff you heard on the radio to boost morale. The air raids were infrequent and rare whilst she was there but it was a massive adrenaline rush, running out to the shelter in the middle of the night, usually nothing happening, better safe than sorry. The war was thankfully turning but still a long way to go.

She received letters from her mother and Jimmie even scrawled a page or two, attached to it. It was the same old, same old, the routine of her mother never changing, mention of her father condensed to 'dad sends his love'. She knew he'd be out with the band playing. That would never stop along with his drinking and other excesses.

She'd heard Kate crying a lot particularly at night. Kate rarely mentioned James but there were photographs of him in every room and his bedroom was virtually untouched, more resembling a shrine. Audrey had the feeling that Kate knew it was all a big mistake, that James would just come walking through the door some day.

Audrey came down the stairs. She'd been reading upstairs, Kate had bought her some books, she'd bought her a lot of things. Kate fussed over her all the time, Ken was always smiling and joking with her making her laugh. She read another letter from her mother, just the same, it was like a carbon copy every letter: everything was fine, her father was fine, she was fine, Jimmie was fine. She doubted if anything was fine. She helped Kate in the kitchen, she peeled some potatoes; it was tinned meat tonight, there was rationing but Ken seemed to have contacts, and they wanted for nothing. He'd even managed to get her some boiled sweets.

Audrey had been there for three weeks now. Her mother had made no mention of her coming back, Kate had not mentioned the subject either. She'd taken Audrey to the local Roman Catholic Chapel the previous Sunday. That was an event. It seemed to go on forever, waving a lot of smoke around and speaking a lot in Latin. Kate had gone to confession, Audrey just sat and waited in the aisle. She said hello to one of the priests, he smiled back at her not speaking. The service seemed to go on forever, she was getting cramp in her legs, she had been getting bored with it all, it seemed to go on forever. In Scotland she rarely ever went to church, just the odd wedding. Her father never went. They'd been made to go to Sunday School which was basically just somebody going over the 'good book' telling them some stories, the Ten Commandments being a popular one, telling you how if you stepped out of line you'd be off to Hell not Heaven.

Audrey missed her mother but she liked being here. Ken was out most of the week and all she did was help Kate out during the day. She sometimes got to see some of the local girls at night and at the weekends; this was turning into a holiday.

She had gone to the cinema on Friday night with two of the other girls in the street. They had been showing the 'Wizard of Oz'. She had enjoyed it, it was a good story. She'd been to the cinema before in Scotland, wished she could go more often.

The cinema was a ten minute bus ride from the street, not like home where it was a good twenty mile drive. They had giggled and laughed all the way through the film, constantly being warned by the cinema usher and other members of the public. The cinema was full of young couples – they seemed to congregate in the darkest spots in the cinema hall, for obvious reasons.

Her new friends seemed to only want to talk about boys and she went along with it. She thought of Jimmie and what he'd be up to, probably kicking a ball around somewhere. They were all about the same age, the other girls going on about kissing boys, their boyfriends, how long they'd been seeing each other, their boyfriends, how they'd like to get married. They both talked about their older brothers, two of whom were getting ready for the big invasion. It seemed like another world in comparison to home, raids happened occasionally, walking around she could see servicemen and women of all the services, but she also saw the wounded and the devastation the bombing had done, the horrors of the war that she had been cocooned from. Although there was rationing in the country rural areas always had the land to live off. Ken had turned his garden into a vegetable patch; he also had an allotment, all part of the ongoing war effort.

The only part of the war she had seen back home was troops training in the local area. They had built a military base, the troops trained on the rough rural terrain. They had also built a POW camp which seemed to be filling all the time with both German and Italian POWs.

Her and Jimmie had gone into the local town which served as sea port for transport to Ireland but also merchant ships and fishing boats. There were little village ports all around the area catering for fishing boats, now there was a permanent military naval presence. The worry of U boats by the locals a piece of local paranoia, particularly at the start of the war they seemed invincible.

When the showing was over the girls all went back to their respective homes, shouting good night at each other. When she entered the house she took her coat off in the hall. She could hear the radio in the background. All the curtains were shut as it was dark outside, Kate and Ken listening to the radio, Kate sewing, Ken smoking his pipe and reading a book, all quiet and tranquil. The contrast of being in Scotland and here, she felt safe and secure here though she did prefer the countryside, she missed her mother, Jimmie, her friends, even her father.

They all had tea and some sponge cake, then she disappeared off to bed, started thinking of a boyfriend for herself, thinking of the boys at her old school, thinking of her friends as she dozed off.

The following week brought news from Scotland; Elizabeth was coming down. Her sister would check on Jimmie and Dermot, see that they could cope on their own. Jimmie would be left to deal with the beasts more than likely.

Her mother arrived on the train. She was planning on staying a week, nothing had been mentioned about her returning. Audrey had been here a month now.

Her mother looked gaunt and tired; she blamed the long journey. She cuddled her mother, Kate hugged and kissed her too, they made their way back to the house.

Her mother just gave it the standard waffle about what was happening back home just the usual how everything was great, nothing bad happening, believe that if you will.

They spent the week just in the usual routine, but it was obvious she was going back. Her mother said little to her when they were on their own, just the standard cover-up. Audrey shared the bed with her mother, her mother was black and blue, normal service had been resumed.

They had one nice day out together: Elizabeth, Kate and Audrey. They went to a local park. Audrey liked the swings. She watched the swans and ducks swim in the park pond. Although still February, a bright sunny day in February 1945. They had packed jam sandwiches and flasks of tea, went to a cafe on the way back for more tea, the war won on tea.

The three were all smiles, even Elizabeth managing to laugh, the tears came when the goodbyes had to be said and it was the long journey home.

4

Dermot and Elizabeth

Dermot had been born in 1901 to what are known as Irish Travellers today, Tinkers back then (well at least Dermot's father was a tinker). They tended to follow the work, seasonal farm labour and also scrap metal, they lived in families. Dermot's forefathers had probably done much the same. A lot had been forced off the land in the way of progress, large estates run on a commercial basis, less labour intensive, the potato famine still fresh in the memory.

Dermot's father had been born into this community, his mother had not. She'd been born to local rural Ulster shopkeepers of Presbyterian protestant descent. Ireland at the time ruled by Britain, to change soon. The Tinkers took little part in any of the troubles. Dermot's father did deals with anyone he could make money with. The industrial protestant north suited him fine; his wife with contacts on one side, he the other side of the divide, work was easier to find. Dermot's father liked trips to Scotland and Wales, sometimes the North of England, contacts everywhere, smuggling another source of income. The old man had what they call 'the gift of the gab'. He spoke native Irish, something he liked to remind everybody of.

Dermot tended to spend the majority of his childhood in Ulster in various camps. He'd been born in a caravan. He'd probably only ever left the province on a handful of occasions. Dermot had been christened a Protestant, his elder sister Kate a Roman Catholic. This was to keep everyone happy, though it did bring in its own unique problems.

Dermot had no interest in learning, his sister Kate showed an aptitude for it. Kate would use this as her ticket in later life; she had ambitions of her own, to get out of here, life in a big city. She got her wish in later life doing secretarial work, ending up in Derby meeting Ken, marrying him, being looked after and spoiled, having James. She always said Englishmen were soft but that was a good thing in her eyes.

Dermot's interests consisted of dealing with horses. This resulted in him going into blacksmithing, in those days a skilled and professional trade. Dermot liked working with the horses. It was more like a vocation, it brought out his gentler side. He liked football and played in goal. He was never that skilled with his feet but had taken to attending a local club in one of the villages as a teenager. He was built tall and strong so he was a natural for the position plus his other passion, boxing. Had come in handy when players on the other team had gotten a bit fresh.

Boxing was popular with the travelling community. Dermot had a gift for this, but his temper had cost him dear. He was constantly being told to calm down by the so-called fight experts, but Dermot's style was to go into a rage. It was effective but not pretty, he was a brawler not a boxer. He was also a fan of the accordion and had been taught by one of the other travellers. It came in handy getting into pubs. Dermot had seen the effect of the 'Great War' on both sides of the communities in Ulster, many sons never returning, others suffering from horrendous physical scars, others mental – what was termed 'Battle Fatigue'.

His mother had ended up marrying his father in unsavoury circumstances. It had been an unholy alliance, a shotgun wedding, marrying a tinker unthinkable but she ran away and got married to him by a priest. She was five months gone. The homecoming had been none too friendly, more a domestic war, her mother and father spitting fire, the shame of it all, her elder brother in a fury about the whole affair. But the dice had been cast the wedding done and Kate born and christened a Catholic. Her mother finally came round, a baby has that effect, and her mother visited in secret until Dermot was born. Then her father took an interest. The boy was christened in the Protestant faith. That was the price of peace.

Dermot had started entering competitions at agricultural shows for blacksmithing; he won quite a few of the big ones. He also entered a lot of boxing matches for cash, he had an aptitude for that as well. Dermot had also got work playing his button-box accordion in the local bars. He'd become friends with some of the local fiddlers and they trawled the bars playing for tips, this and free drink. It was easy money, as far as he was concerned a free night out.

His father had become a deranged alcoholic over the years steadily getting worse. He had a violent streak. Thankfully he kept it under control, until they carted him off to the local asylum and that was the last they saw of him. He'd tried to kill Elizabeth in a rage in full public view. They visited him every few months but it seemed pointless. He didn't recognise any visitors, just rambled on nonsensically. By this time Kate had gone to England, so Dermot was alone in the caravan with his mother. He'd been noticed at the shows of being a competent blacksmith and been offered work in Galloway, Scotland. It was time to make a move. The money promised more than Ulster, more a steady stream plus accommodation. He was going and that was it, his mind made up.

Scotland

Dermot arrived in Scotland in 1920. Things were and had been kicking off big time in what was to be known as the Republic of Ireland, it was probably a good time to go. His mother could move back with her parents who were still alive so she'd be well provided for. The conflict on the island of Ireland was escalating; bitterness on both sides. Dermot wanted out. He was stuck in the middle: northern Protestant mother and southern Catholic father, a mongrel.

Dermot came across on a fishing trawler. He'd met some of the fishermen in the local bars. He discovered he wasn't a natural sailor and had no sea legs, just grabbed onto a fixed seat and let the other men get on with their jobs. He was sick a lot, they kept telling him what 'guid' weather they were having. He was freezing and steadily getting soaked as the sea water sprayed over the deck. He was not suited for the sea, a black suit and wool jersey were no match for the fishermen's gear. He also hated the salty smell of the sea and look of the fish; it was enough to put him off eating fish.

He'd been initially offered a job for a local landowner, horses used as a mainstay in agricultural, also a pastime for the landed gentry – fox hunting and such – with hunts scattered all over the area of Southern Scotland.

He never ever saw the local Lord or Laird and dealt predominately with the Estate Manager. The estate consisted of a lot of land, with sections used for grouse and pheasant shooting, but also land rented out to tenant farmers who basically got a cottage and piece of land which they farmed. Dermot had seen this in the extreme in Ireland, it seemed to be a fairer deal here though, with the majority of people happier here than in Ireland.

He liked dealing with the Clydesdales and on the estate there were several teams he dealt with. He'd become popular with his fellow workers and the locals he'd met; he'd been given a room in a cottage on the estate and shared it with two other men. They dealt with the gardens. The cottage had three bedrooms a bathroom (indoors with bath) and living room and kitchen containing a small stove and fire. This meant hot water (a luxury). As a member of the staff they all got free bed and board, meals served in a staff dining room attached to the kitchen; life was good.

Some of the men would go to the local village which was a couple of miles away, usually at weekends or when there was a dance in the local hall. The village had four little bars. The action though was when the local dances were held. He had met a couple of fiddlers in one of the bars, asked if they'd like an accordionist to join them, and that was it: a supply of free drink at the weekends.

Dermot had become friends with a lot of the household staff, especially the female ones. They loved his accent, and he was tall dark and handsome and full of the charms. Sexual relationships between the staff were frowned upon, but it happened all the time. Dermot was particularly keen on a Highland girl called Emily. He'd had girlfriends back in Ireland, all with the travelling community, but he'd been careful as he'd been caught in the woods in the act with a girl called Mary Miligan. The trouble was she had four brothers, all as mad as each other. When word got out he got a beating he wouldn't forget in a long time, three holding him as the other got laid into him. This was done in a rotational fashion. They'd made him black and blue, and smashed one of his hands in the process. This rendered him useless, no blacksmithing, accordion or boxing. Thankfully his mother always had spare cash.

He'd got his own back on the eldest Miligan months later, lying in wait for him of a night, breaking his jaw with one punch but also breaking all the fingers in his right hand one by one. After this the other brothers seemed to avoid him like the plague. This suited him fine. He'd moved up the pecking order so they could all fuck off. There was always resentment with the other travellers, him and his mother the prods. The sarcastic remarks that his mother had driven her man mad, well fuck them fuck the lot of them.

He'd been meeting Emily late at night, he knew the gardeners knew but he suspected the gamekeepers would know too. They were always raking around at night, looking for poachers, a swift kicking administered to the poacher if caught. Sometimes though a financial inducement from the poachers could grease palms. It wouldn't do for the hounds to kill all the foxes. What would the hounds do?

They met in a clearing in a little copse in the garden, at least in the summer too cold in winter. No one ever around after ten p.m., Dermot always took a blanket. He got her into the cottage when he knew the others weren't going to be around, bribery sometimes to get them out of the place. They all had separate rooms but the walls were paper thin, too thin for what Dermot and Emily wanted.

Dermot was always full of lust when he got Emily on her own. He was lying in bed thinking of what he'd done with her. He'd gotten the other two out for the night. They'd decided to do some extra work in the greenhouses, it meant a half-day for them both the day after. Dermot had smuggled her in, pulled her dress up. She had no underwear on. He hadn't even bothered to kiss her yet, he pulled down his trousers and pants and penetrated her roughly. He'd been hard waiting for her.

He took her in doggy fashion, still fully clad. She was wet and excited. She moaned with delight. He wanted to shoot his seed. He pulled out his cock and shot his load over her. He entered her again and repeated the action though this time he hammered her hard and fingered her anus at the same time. After he had finished himself he stripped himself and her naked, they climbed into the bed, her buttocks drenched in sperm. He massaged her whilst kissing her he ended up going down on her for an age. She moaned loudly as she climaxed, then they just held each other saying nothing. Emily told him she loved him, Dermot grunted his approval.

The following week was one of the dances organised by the Masonic Lodge. Emily couldn't go, apparently a party in the 'big house'. Emily was needed for work. Dermot was reluctant to go, it was organised by the masons. Though Dermot was a Protestant he had no truck with the theory that Catholics were inferior. He wasn't a fan of any of the secret societies on the go, Catholic or Protestant, there were plenty to choose from.

There seemed to be revolutions all over in Russia, Mexico and even Ireland. It interested him not in the slightest, keep your head down and look after yourself, fuck them all. The revolutions had seen the West of Scotland and Glasgow in particular become a hotbed for left wing political groups, union and labour movements and all that went with it, marches galore, bands playing – a time for change.

He instead went to a little bar in the village which he liked: 'The Judges Keep'. He was their goalkeeper in the local leagues; they were always struggling to get a keeper so when he'd said he could play in goal he was an automatic selection. His technique was much as in Ireland, thumping the hell out of the opposition, the warning that scoring against him may lead to swift retribution later on. He was a bad loser and had a temper to match.

He walked the route down to the pub. It was an old country lane really leading to the village, covered in cow and horseshit. Manoeuvring through it was easy in daylight, harder when drunk in darkness, just the lights from the big estate house to guide you in. Autumn was nearly upon them and there was a real chill in the air, it had been raining early. It rained all the time here, just like Ireland.

He met some of the locals he knew and got into a round of drinks. The bars in those days never saw women, the women congregated at the dances. That was their chance to shine. The dances could go on late as well, local police turning a blind eye as long as everyone behaved. Alcohol was sold at some dances, at others not. The dance tonight was supposedly tee total. Highly unlikely, as drink was easily smuggled in, and the majority of men were well lubricated upon arrival.

Dermot was having a grand old time. He was on his eighth pint of heavy and seemed to have taken a liking to the local whisky. He found it harsher tasting than the Irish, he sometimes managed to get himself poteen from the Irish travellers when they passed through. The Laird allowed them access to his land and in general they behaved themselves; they were for the Laird though a cheap source of seasonal labour for crops needing picked, 'tattie hoking' and such.

Dermot had had enough and he had to shoe some horses first thing in the morning, so he said his goodbyes, but was press ganged into having another pint and nip before departing, always room for one more.

He went past the local hall to see what was happening. He didn't fancy going in. He saw some of the local lads. He went over to see them and get a light. He'd taken to smoking when he arrived in Scotland but only when he had a drink in him, cigarettes always untipped. He coughed away. He wasn't a natural smoker but he liked the image of the hard man, the heavy drinker, smoker and hitter.

The local lads were trying to persuade Dermot to come in. He succumbed to temptation and had a slug from a half-bottle one of the lads had. They all paid the entrance fee, the money collected in a tin by a couple of old timers. The hall was loud and smoky, all the young men on one side of the hall, the girls on the other. Some dance band playing the traditional Scottish stuff. There were lots of older adults there keeping an eye on the boys and girls, no funny business, no hanky panky, everyone on their best behaviour. Dermot had another cigarette: this was boring and he was tired. He decided to leave.

Stevie Muir was shouting at him,

"Oh, aye, ya fuck'n micks cannae handle yir drink, tawdle of back hame."

Stevie had a big mouth when he was drunk which had gotten him into bother before. The rest of his friends knew he was in bother now. Dermot usually tended to let it pass, but he'd enough of him. He went over to him, said nothing, grabbed his arm and rammed it up behind his back. He squealed, his friends all backed off, Dermot still said nothing. Actions do speak louder than words, he thought. He frog marched Stevie outside past the people on the door. He even managed to shout, "Night folks."

He took Stevie round the back of the hall. Stevie was pleading with him, telling him it was a joke, a misunderstanding. Dermot reached a clearing and spun him round. he cracked him hard once on the nose. Stevie was on his arse with a broken nose stunned and pleading for it all to stop Dermot was about to lay the boot in, but stopped when he heard crying from a lane leading back into a small wood. He looked and was transfixed. He told Stevie to scram, which he duly did. Stevie was terrified, there'd be no more of his lip that was for sure. Dermot shouted at him, "Never call me a mick again ya wee bastard!"

That would be unlikely. Dermot went over to the girl. She was petite and pretty, Dermot towered over her. She had a polka dot dress on and tiny little black shoes. She had shoulder length black wavy hair, she didn't wear makeup. Dermot tried to square himself up. He was unsure if she had seen what had just happened, hopefully not. He smiled at her as she looked at him, he spoke.

"Are yeh awright? Yeh look cald."

"What'd yeh hit him fir?"

Christ she did see him.

"He owed me money and wouldnae pay." He lied

"You didnae need to hit him."

"What's yir name?"

"Elizabeth."

"Mine's Dermot."

They made small talk. Dermot told her about himself, embellishing it with a few half-truths and a good few lies. She told him she worked for her father with her sister, he owned the local bakers. Dermot knew where it was. She lived next to it in a house, again with her father, mother and sister. It started to drizzle, Dermot said he'd walk her home – it was only a few minutes away. He went up the old cobbled main street of the village and said goodbye at her door, he saw lights on inside the house.

"I might see yeh again."

"Yeh might indeed!"

She smiled at him as she shut the door. He headed back down the road heading down the main street, hearing the music from the hall, some loiterers outside. He cut off down the lane, a couple of miles walk in the rain, it would sober him up. He lit a cigarette and smoked. Yes indeed he might see this Elizabeth again, she was sweet.

Dermot had gotten back about midnight, just crashed out on his bed fully clothed.

He got up early. They had a stove in the cottage. They only usually used it for making tea; they would go to the big house kitchens for food. Dermot made some tea and splashed some water on his face. He had changed in his work clothes, hung up his good stuff after giving it a brush.

The three of them had an indoor toilet and bath. This was luxury to Dermot, though he'd never admit it to any of the others. Outside toilets, tin baths were a way of life for him. He'd always brushed his teeth diligently, his mother had got him into good hygiene habits; his father had tended to let himself go as the years had passed though. Thankfully, not a trait Dermot would pick up on.

Dermot felt rough. He had a bottle of whisky in his bedroom. He poured some into the tea as a pick me up. He went to the smithy on the estate, past the gardens, no life there yet.

He started the smithy fire. He soon had it roaring, the anvil and all his tools laid out. One of the tenant farmers had two horses needing shoed; it would take a few hours.

The farmer arrived on time and Dermot went to work. He pulled up the horses hooves, checked the sizes. He had some pre-made but would have to do a few minor alterations. Cleaning the hooves as he went along, holding the hoof between his legs the horse facing one way Dermot the opposite, always careful when dealing with the hind legs, no need for a set of broken ribs or broken back. He used the fire to heat the horseshoes and made a few adjustments. He then doused them in cold water and nailed them on.

The farmer thanked him. Dermot had a kettle lowered onto the fire, he made some tea for himself and the farmer, they both drank out of old tin mugs, no milk just sugar. The farmer was telling Dermot how hard things had been lately for him and his wife. His son had come back from the war minus an arm and with shell shock. Dermot had never met him but had heard stories; the others said he was mad. Dermot had seen a lot of it with the returnees in Ireland. It was even sadder, though, when whole streets of young men not much older than himself had been killed. His father had always said die for your country, for what? Perhaps his old father had a point, none of these lads had come home to much. I suppose at least they'd made it back. The Laird's son had been killed in one of the main battles of the War, Dermot couldn't remember what one, there had been so many. People talked sometimes of another war, who knew what the future would bring.

Dermot went back to the cottage. Emily might pop in later under some pretence. She'd been working late last night so she wouldn't have to start till lunchtime. Dermot had said he'd give the gardeners a hand later on in the day if he had time.

He lay in bed. He saw a letter from his mother sitting on his dresser. It had lain unopened for over a week; he knew it would just be the same old news. He thought a lot about the future, perhaps he should move on, he'd been here for over six months, he was getting restless. He'd managed to save quite a bit of money. His meals and board were free and he'd even made a little playing with the fiddlers though that tended to pay for whisky and mischief. Dermot had thought about emigrating. There seemed to be life in other places. He thought of America a lot, the land of opportunity. He liked reading westerns and about America, it all seemed so wild and free, the land of opportunity. Loads of Irish were heading there; the Scots seemed to be heading for Canada in droves. Even Australia and New Zealand appealed. He had a good set of hands and could turn his hand to anything, he could even drive now, he'd got one of the porters in the big house to take him out in old van they had for bringing in supplies. He was multi-talented. He'd also been thinking of this Elizabeth, the baker's daughter.

He dozed off. Emily hadn't shown, he'd go and see how the gardeners were getting on, he'd heard them leaving earlier when he was half-dozing. He liked the crack with the lads. He jumped up and headed for the garden. He still had his work clothes on, he put his boots on.

Dermot shouted at one of the maids, she was skiving off with a cigarette hanging out of her mouth, smoking behind the bins at the back kitchen door. She waved back.

Dermot arrived at the garden. The lads were at the vegetable garden, they were turning over the soil. This was too get the nutrients to the surface or some gardening bollocks, probably give them something to do. They threw a shovel at him. They were called Archie and Colin; they came from someplace up north. Why they were here was a mystery. Surely plenty of bigger jobs up North, Dermot had said. Need to get away, they replied.

"So, look whit the cat dragged in."

"Whit were yeh up tae last night?"

"Back late rattling around."

"Nae bit of fluff though Dermot, yir losing yir touch."

Dermot told them to shut up, did so with a big grin. He was getting hungry though, had missed breakfast and lunch due to last night's activities.

"Onnae food, you two?"

"Aye, there are some sandies in the greenhouse. Help yirself."

"You'll hae tae work fir yir supper though."

"Fuck off!"

Dermot went to the greenhouse. It was massive. In the summer months it was great, filled with tomatoes and cucumbers, not much here in the autumn though.

Dermot returned after eating the sandwiches.

"Onnae tea?"

"Only if you make it… ya lazy bastard, tell us where yeh were."

Dermot told them what he'd been up to but omitted his encounter with Elizabeth. The three yabbled on about football, the upcoming games. They all played in the same team.

The local fairground was coming round, would be in the town in a few weeks. They'd have to all go in for a night, get the bus into town, or arrange a lift. Dermot knew a lot of these lot who ran the fairgrounds or 'the shows' as they were known; a lot of them were Irish or descended from Ireland. Basically travellers, wouldn't surprise him if he was related in some distant way. He'd always fancied working in the summer at the fairground, plenty of fun, plenty of girls, not a real job. Dermot went and had his dinner with Archie and Colin. He was bushed. No sign of Emily. He headed off to bed.

The Old Man

Dermot had had his breakfast and was working at the smithy fixing some gates for the Estate Manager. One of the porters came up to him said the Estates Manager was wanting him. What fuck'n now? thought Dermot. He entered his office.

The boss told him to sit down. Very cordial, Dermot thought, was he up for the sack? The boss said there'd been a call for him in the middle of the night. His father had died and he was to return home. Dermot was told to go for the week, they'd be able to cope without him. He gave him a week's pay in advance.

So Dermot headed to home back on the ferry this time, easier on the stomach. He'd said his goodbyes. Emily had been in tears. He'd gotten a lift into town with one of the porters. I think everybody thought he wouldn't come back, but he had every intention of coming back.

He went to his mother's. She was back with her parents, still alive; she was running a little shop that sold knickknacks and such. He said hello to Granddad and Grandma McNally, he'd always gotten on well with them, even though they hated his father though it wasn't the fact they hated him that irked them. It was the fact that he'd married their daughter, him a Catholic to boot.

His mother held him. Kate was out walking, she'd arrived the night before on an earlier ferry.

His mother told him he'd died of a stroke. It was quick. The funeral had been all arranged, everything arranged she kept saying. The coffin had already been delivered to the chapel.

71

Dermot thought, not burning him in his caravan. Dermot smiled. The old bastard, he hadn't been that good but not bad either, just an old cunt.

He hadn't seen Kate in over a year. He missed her, she was to be getting married, now living in Derby, living in sin as well. He'd been her landlord, one for the church that, give them all something to talk about.

She told him about Kenneth, how he'd have to come and visit. Kate hit him after he joked did she do it to get a reduction in rent. He was ten years her senior, but she seemed much in love, so he was happy for her. She asked him about what was happening, he responded in his usual way with no information volunteered.

The funeral was in the Catholic church. The only member of his mother's family to attend was his grandma. Going to a Catholic church was taboo for a member of the Protestant community. He had gone up the night before to see the coffin. It was open casket on a trolley. He looked at his father, resplendent in good suit. Kate was in praying, talking with the priest, Dermot the outsider in here.

At the funeral Dermot stood at the entrance of the chapel shaking the hands of those who attended, coming to pay their respects (get drunk afterwards). He recognised some but not all. His uncle stood with him. He had come up from the South.

The priest gave the service, said mass, offered confession to anyone who wanted it. It was one of the few times Dermot had been in a chapel, usually christenings, weddings and funerals. It dragged on, a lot of it in Latin, for fuck sake get on with it.

Confession... Confess...! The bastards in here would be there all day.

They carried the coffin to the graveyard. The priest had asked Dermot if he'd like to say a few words. Dermot said no he'd let his uncle do the honours. It was a big turnout, all the tinker community, a good hundred plus. A lot of the women were crying, his mother and Kate dry-eyed. His mother had probably shed enough tears over the years.

There was to be a few drinks at the tinker site, they were invited, his mother wouldn't go. Kate and him went, walked to the site. It seemed to have expanded. He met a load of his old mates, old enemies too, they had a big bonfire going, drink freely passed around, bottles of beer, whisky, gin and poteen.

Everyone was passing on their respects to himself and Kate. Kate changed so much, smartly dressed, sexy even, she was a city girl now, looking like a star.

He and Kate were now the outsiders. They chatted amongst themselves, they both knew they'd likely never be back here. Kate would never lower herself, he thought.

He thought about Emily, also Elizabeth, he'd be glad to get back.

He drank more beer. The music had started, accordions and fiddles; this would be an all night affair, probably going on a good few days. Raise a glass and all that shite to the great man.

Dermot asked Kate if she wanted to go. She was fine, she drank but moderately, Dermot hammered into it. Fuck it, he thought, I'll only bury one father. He was up dancing for a while, Kate just laughing, laughing at him acting the arse. They both ended up leaving. Dermot didn't know what time it was. His mother had given him his father's watch after he'd been committed, but he never used it, always scared he'd lose it.

By the time they got back Dermot just slept in the armchair beside the fire. Kate went up to her bedroom, Dermot couldn't be arsed. He fell asleep, awoke with a blanket round him. He'd be glad to get going, say his goodbyes.

He had breakfast, not much. Kate and himself said they'd stay another night and then go. They just sat the five of them, never any mention of wills or inheritance, all that taken care of when he went to the funny farm. They played cards in the afternoon, constantly drinking tea, his Grandpa and Grandma kept a dry house. The day passed quickly. They had a nice roast dinner and he drifted off thinking of his mother and father, Kate, and all of his friends; that was in the past though.

Before he knew it he was on the ferry. It had taken over an hour to get to Larne for the ferry. Kate and he had said little. They arrived into Stranraer (the toon as it was known by locals), Kate was getting the train from the harbour. He waited with her till her train arrived, waited till she left. Kate was crying, telling him to visit, he promised he would, he'd better attend the wedding when they got round to it. It was a dry, cold day but he decided to walk back to the estate. It was four miles, he'd be there quick enough. He missed Kate, he missed her terribly, he wanted her close, she had always been there for him…God he missed her.

When he arrived back the lads were out. He made some tea, went to the office of the estate manager, said he'd be back tomorrow. That was fine, condolences all round. He'd only been gone four days. It all seemed too surreal so fast, one minute alive one minute dead. He wished he'd spent more time with his mother; it was not to be.

Emily came to see him, she was crying away, fuck sake all I need he thought, another crying woman, he'd had to deal with a few after the funeral. What he needed was some carnal activity, and with the lads out working this was what he was going to get. They were at it all afternoon; they went for dinner at the big house leaving the cottage separately.

He sat with the lads, all condolences from everyone, all the staff even the ones he didn't know or like: the chefs, the maids, the porters, the waiters. He told Archie and Colin to get their skates on at dinner, get back to the cottage, he had a surprise. Emily was working tonight, no that wasn't the surprise.

Dermot got back and produced four large pint bottles of lemonade.

"Fuck'n great, who's got the tea and scones?"

Archie and Colin not impressed till Dermot informed them it was poteen.

"Fuck me!" was the response.

The three of them got some mugs. Archie and Colin had never tried it before; after a few swigs they could hardly talk, their throats both on fire. Dermot was used to it, he had a cigarette hanging out his mouth. Careful you don't blow yourself up.

The three of them pissed, Colin telling them how he was shagging one of the chambermaids, Colin taking the piss out of Archie calling him a big poof. All of them agreeing that Helen the chambermaid was in need of a good fuck and that Colin was just the boy to do the job.

"Archie is a poofter. Nah! Nah! Nah! Archie is a poofter Nah! Nah! Nah!"

"Fuck off ya bastards."

In a drunken stupor Dermot told them about Elizabeth, a prize catch.

"Yeh'll be okay fir cake?"

"It's mare than cake I'm after, I'll be gaein her the cream."

Dermot on his bragging rights now,

"Fuck you'se all ya fuckers."

Dermot into meltdown now, past the point of caring, Archie and Colin following suit, Dermot producing his button box accordion, a load of the old stuff belting out, the talk centring on women and sport, Rangers versus Celtic, boxing, the Yanks and America.

The night would be quick; the morning would come even quicker, a nice hangover for all three of the cowboys.

Fairground Fun

The weeks rolled on. It was getting colder, the nights drawing in as they said, stormy days and nights more common, Archie and Colin complaining of the cold, Dermot staying near the blacksmiths fire. Dermot wore nothing more than light weight trousers and a vest half the time.

The fairground had arrived; it was here for a few weeks. The three amigos had decided to go at the weekend and make a night of it, they could tadge a lift in and hopefully back. Emily and two of her girlfriends, Fiona and Maggie, had opted to come along. Her two friends were maids of some sort in the house. Archie and Colin would have their hands full if they played their cards right.

They got a lift from one of the porters. He lived in town and had access to a van, it wasn't luxury but it would do. There was a late bus running to the village so they could get that to get back to the estate.

When they arrived they could hear the screams. The fair had some rides such as big wheel (not that big, thought Dermot), waltzer, tests of strength, lots of food being sold, the smell of toffee apples, candyfloss, bottles of lemonade and other drinks. They also had a boxing booth. Interesting, thought Dermot.

They went on the rides together. Colin and Archie looked to have cracked it, back to the cottage for some fun, still some poteen left, the lads had gotten a case of beer in as well.

The girls screamed on the rides, Dermot thought what the fuck on the waltzer, his guts churning, wishing he hadn't eaten so much rubbish, glad to get off the fuck'n thing.

"Yeh okay, Dermot? Yir looking shaky."

"Fuck off."

The boys did the hammer, a test of strength, Dermot refused.

"I hammer metal all day."

Dermot was eyeing up the boxing booth. The girls had all gone to the toilets (or down a dark alley opposite where the fairground was). Dermot had looked in to the booth: about twenty of the locals some of the travellers, he recognised none. Dermot found out what the score was: last three rounds with the bruiser and the pot of cash was yours. Dermot had looked at the opposition, an old ring hand by the look of him, covered in scars, probably not all from boxing. It had been a while since he'd been

77

in the ring, he was still fit, he had to be with the job he did. Time for some fun then he thought, let's see what this old bastard is made of.

The girls waited outside. No place for a woman.

Dermot got the gloves on, Archie and Colin giving him advice.

"Punch the fuck out of him, Dermot!"

Dermot was ready for action. He jumped into the ring, down to his vest now, gloves on, touch gloves with the old guy and away we go, one of the tinks the referee.

The old man knew the tricks. He had fast feet, he'd jabbed Dermot left right a few times, no discernable style. Dermot felt the sting, remembered the feeling, instinct slipping in. He was immune to the noise. Archie and Colin screaming away, some of the locals the worse for wear screaming their lungs out. The bell rung; first round was over.

"One down, two to go. Hang in there, Dermot. Nothing fancy."

Dermot had decided he was going to floor him the second round. The old guy looked tired, his face said it all, scarred and worn out. Dermot went in with an old combination of punches, he then just went into a rage, just throwing punches consistently. The old guy knew how to defend, how to get out of trouble, Dermot put him on his arse, but he was up on the count of six. Fuck it.

"Just hang in there, ya daft cunt."

The third round, it consisted of the old man just surviving, Dermot jabbing him consistently, Dermot trying to box not brawl. The bell went, no knockout for Dermot. The old man nodded at him. Dermot got his pot of gold. The tinkers not pleased their man had lost, Dermot telling them it's good for business, got to see somebody winning apart from their man.

Dermot then got a verbal grilling, they'd heard him string a sentence together, Dermot had heard of some of them. White was their name, they were spearing the arse of a tin can now, just questions, time to go.

"If yir ever looking for work."

"I'll keep it in mind, thanks."

No chance, he thought. Dermot took the boys and girls to the shooting gallery, he was on a roll, Archie and Colin having a go, Dermot missing every time his eyesight fading, Archie winning a big teddy bear.

"Fuck'n suits yeh."

Archie gave it to Maggie. He'd been sniffing round her all night.

"C'mon. I'm buying."

The drinks were on Dermot then. A little bar at the sea front, women a new for the bar, Dermot insisting, the three lads have pints and chasers, fuck it you're only young once. Dermot thought about the fight, his face was stinging, the drink helped numb it, his ribs would be bruised in the morning. He should have killed the old cunt. He bought the girls gin and lime. The place was dead. They had another round, Dermot buying. Let's get the ten thirty p.m. bus.

"C'mon, we've got some drink at the cottage."

Everyone agreed, slightly high on the alcohol. They all jumped on the bus. It was practically empty, everyone would be getting the last one after eleven p.m. The bus rattled along, they sat up the back. The pairing off had happened, Archie and Colin were in there. Good effort from the boys, no slacking.

They got off in the village and walked briskly back up the well worn path, drinking and shagging on their minds, at least that was the boys' intention. The fire in the cottage was still going, they kept it on all the time just chucking logs and coal on to it. It was linked to a boiler, hot water.

Dermot poured out the poteen, they had some mugs, the case of beer appeared, the girls sticking to the beer, the boys having both, just a load of old wooden chairs. Dermot had Emily on his knee, the other two soon following suit with their intended conquests. Dermot disappeared first to the toilet then to bed with Emily in tow, time for some shagging. She had all her clothes off and was under the sheets, Dermot mounting her and riding her hard, shooting his load over her tits, rubbing it in. He could hear Colin at it with his new bit of fluff, they were banging away like an artillery gun, she was a screamer. He heard Emily dozing, he listened in till he could hear no more, he drifted off.

Things that happen

A few days later Emily arrived at the smithy. She was crying her eyes out, her father had died, she had decided she was going back up north to be with her mother for the time being. Was she coming back, Dermot thought, probably not, in fact certainly not. She'd be helping out the mother. By the sound of it her mother ran the tenant farm, her father a waster but still her father all the same. He held her for a long time.

They agreed they'd write. Dermot doubted it, he wasn't inclined to write to anyone, Kate and his mother the exception and that was laboured.

He went to the station with her. She had taken everything she had, saying she might be back, a change from definitely back within the space of a day. He was sad to see her go, he told her to look after herself and give her mother his best. Jesus it all seemed so quick, one minute Emily here the next gone, same with her father.

He got back, went to the smithy, finished a few odd jobs, went for dinner, picked up a letter. It was Kate's handwriting, wonder what was up, he hadn't had a letter from her in a few months.

He went back and read a book he'd gotten, a western. He dozed off, made himself some tea, the gruesome twosome were nowhere to be seen, probably off with their latest flames. He opened Kate's letter, always the same fancy writing paper, read it once had to read it again. He'd need to respond.

Kate, unmarried to Ken, but now three months pregnant. Wow, his mother would not be pleased. It was what Kate wanted though, she'd always wanted a child. The two of them had got married the previous weekend. Kate had got half her wish, Dermot knew she never wanted a big wedding. The less contact Kate had with the Irish family contingent the better, no embarrassing moments at the wedding for Kate. Kate was telling him that she loved Ken. Dermot knew she was on to a good thing, he'd never met Ken but he seemed like a good man, someone who'd never abuse her, someone who'd always put her first. Dermot wondered if she'd informed Ireland, their mother would be on the warpath, he could hear her now.

"The shame of it, as if this family hasn't gone through enough."

Dermot got some writing paper. He scribbled out a page congratulating her and Ken, telling her he'd have to visit. He was genuinely pleased for her, she'd bettered herself, gotten away, she'd never be back to Ireland apart from a death. He felt tears well up. He'd wait till the dust had settled before contacting his mother, see what she was saying, maybe she'd be pleased. They were out of sight, out of mind, perhaps she'd never mention it to anyone.

So Emily gone, Kate settled, time he got on with things too.

Elizabeth

Kate had written again, apparently their mother was giving her the silent treatment. Well that was one of the options, better than hitting the roof. Dermot had written his mother a letter, the week before, no response.

Dermot was playing football this Saturday. Archie and Colin would be playing too, so there would be some beverages consumed later on. They were playing some team from a pub down county.

It was a cold day, Dermot felt it standing in goal, the wind was biting into him. The sooner this was over the better. It was a nil nil draw, what a waste of time.

They got changed in the local village hall and headed to the pub. The other team were fucking off, not even bothering coming for a drink. This would be remembered, bad manners. The wankers.

Dermot had a few but popped out, he headed for the bakers. Let's see what opportunism would hold. He hadn't seen her (Elizabeth) in a while, hoped she'd remember him. He walked to the shop and looked in the window to the array of cakes, breads, pies and snacks. He wasn't interested in the food.

She saw him looking in and smiled. He went in. She was serving. He bought a couple of scotch pies, asked her how she was, was she going to the dance next week, yes the reply, he'd see her there then, she probably would was her response and that was it. She asked him where he'd been, so he told her the news. He'd been busy, funeral and all that, he hadn't been out much, had missed the fair (liar). She told him her father had gone to his bed. He baked all night, went to bed early morning. She was in charge of the shop, her mother next door doing the household chores. Dermot said his goodbyes.

Dermot went across the road and sat on the dyke. He watched her, she watched him. There was a connection, he felt it. She was smiling at him. He ate his pies, waved when he left, she waved back. He was on.

He went back to the pub, picked up his stuff. He wasn't intending on staying but ended up there all day till closing time. He'd left his accordion behind the bar, the fiddlers were in so that was them all for the day. The rest of the team left in dribs and drabs, next game next week, training optional Wednesday night. Dermot never bothered going to the training half the time, he was the only choice for keeper, first on the team sheet.

The cottage trio were still there till closing time (when the barman had had enough). They staggered back up the road, all of them relieving themselves on numerous occasions along the way, Colin relieving his stomach as a bonus.

It would be another quick night, work in the morning, fuck he couldn't be bothered. He needed a change. He wanted to be his own man, control his destiny. He was starting to feel like a beast of burden.

"All of them hungover for days…"

"Fuck'n age."

"Fuck off."

The week went in quick, Dermot felt lethargic. He listened at night to music from a gramophone that played up at the big house. They must have had the window open. Dermot was feeling run down. It was just work food sleep, another week going by… gone.

So it was Saturday, the dance at night, this one run by the farmers, a bar at it as well.

Dermot went to the football in the morning, he wasn't in the mood standing between the goalposts, pissing rain. He'd arrived early. They all crammed into the back of a clapped out old van – star quality, smelling of chicken shite. They drove to one of the other villages six miles down the coast.

Some fuck'n church team to boot, no after match drinks. After the game they ran to the van. It was hailstones now. They just wanted to get the fuck away from here, 1–1 the score. They got back to the pub, Dermot had one pint and left. It had cleared up, he didn't want an all-day session, he had other things on his mind for the night, the elusive Elizabeth and if she wasn't up for it then some other floozy.

Dermot had a sleep in the afternoon, Archie and Colin were no shows. They were obviously staying down at the village propping up the bar, drinking for Scotland. Dermot had a quick wash, he had his suit pressed, he'd look the part anyway, he'd be sober too. He poured himself a beer, there was some bottles below the sink in the main room. He looked outside. It had dried up and was still dry. Thank fuck, he could do without getting soaked. He lit a cigarette and set off. It was chilly but dry, hopefully it'd stay that way. He had loaded the fire up with a load of wood and coal, put the fire guard back down, stop sparks burning them all to death.

Dermot set off, hitting a brisk pace, saw a couple of gamekeepers patrolling the fields. Their work never ended, the fuckers had a never-ending supply of game, mind you. Dermot had seen them selling it down the local pubs, chancing bastards.

Dermot arrived. The music was playing, the fiddlers were there. Dermot could have told you who would be there, even where they'd be standing or sitting and how pissed they'd be. Colin was well gone but he always recovered like a champion racehorse down the last furlong. He was propping up the bar humming along to the music. Archie you never knew. He was like a Chinaman, seemed to have an expressionless face when he was drunk or drinking, you never knew if he was drunk or sober. Dermot got four large whiskies, one for each of the lads and two for himself. He had catching up to do. The barman handed him his accordion, it seemed to spend half the time behind the bar here, the other half on the other side of the bar. Dermot played along, he played by ear. He never knew what he was playing half the time, he just followed the harmony.

After a few more and a few more after that they ended up at the dance. They paid the entrance fee and got their hands stamped. It was bustling, all sorts were there: villagers, farmers, farm workers, youth in general, and some old drunkards who should know better.

Dermot looked around, plenty of women in, Dermot nodded at a few ending up talking to some lads he knew from the estate. There was cigarette smoke everywhere, Archie and Colin meeting up with Fiona and Maggie, Dermot always got them mixed up, nice enough girls though.

No sign of Elizabeth. He danced with one of Emily's friends, getting grilled, had he heard from her, yes (he lied) everything fine. He told her he needed the toilet, went outside for a piss but wanted shot of her, hearing about all her problems.

He saw Elizabeth going in at a distance. She looked good, was with a group of her friends. He'd play it cool, he lit up a cigarette smoked it slowly, no rush. He went back in, saw she was drinking, and went over.

"I'll get yeh another."

"I'm fine, thanks."

"A dance then."

He wasn't taking no for an answer had her by the hand and was dragging her on to the dance floor. She was giggling, all her friends watching, Dermot sticking his tongue out at them, making them laugh.

The night went by quick. Dermot was wanting into her knickers but he thought she wasn't the sort of girl to do that. He took her outside and kissed her; she didn't resist but didn't encourage him either. They'd danced all night. Dermot liked her, she was hot stuff, and a little posh too, she reminded him of his mother, her upbringing identical in many ways.

Dermot walked her back to outside her house. She kissed him. She had tomorrow afternoon off, told him to meet her in the village square at two p.m. Okay, he'd make it. The beauty of Dermot's job was he could make his own hours. As long as the work got done no one seemed bothered. She pecked him on the cheek. Two p.m. sharp.

Dermot was smitten. He knocked on the pub window as the door was locked. The barman, looking through the peephole, let him in. A celebration was in order.

Dermot woke about nine a.m., couldn't fully remember how he'd got back, thought he'd come up the road with one of the porters. The gardening duo were still in bed, he could hear the snores, wondered if they were alone. He went to the kitchen in the big house, had some sausages and tea.

He went to the smithy but had no intention of doing terribly much, just pottered around, didn't bother starting a fire. Decided to go and get ready.

The twosome still in bed lazy bastards, Dermot shouted at them both before leaving, the response inevitable.

He made it to the square by one thirty p.m. He was early, loads of church goers coming out, church bells going, only the one Protestant Kirk in the village. Funny, no one had ever asked him what religion he was. The sky was cloudy. Hopefully it wouldn't rain. It was 2.05 p.m. on his pocket watch. Where the fuck was she?

Then she appeared, winter coat and hat. She looked like a star, fuck he should have brought her something. He'd scrubbed his teeth with dental powder, so he should be minty at least.

They went a walk up by the old abbey. It was in ruins but had some sort of historical significance, it looked to have been burnt out. Dermot held her hand. She was a real chatterbox, telling him about her elder sister, her mother, her father, her distant relations, cats and dogs, Christ she could talk for Scotland. Dermot just nodded and said 'Aye' quite a lot. He thought Irish women were bad for talking, Christ this one was endless, however she made him smile and laugh.

She was so petite. Dermot had big calloused hands, rough as sandpaper, she said he should put cream on his hands 'Aye'. Dermot always seemed to have a layer of dirt ingrained on his hands, no matter how much he scrubbed, he had a worker's hands no mistake.

Dermot took her by the hand, led her into the woods, kissed her, and stroked her hair. He wanted to go further but she didn't, she slapped his hands away. She let him hold her hand. He was smitten. He felt gooey and light headed, he'd never felt like this before. She was a catch and he wanted to land her.

Summer 1921

The winter had come and gone it had been fairly mild, a little snow in the area but only in the higher ground, the wind and gales more of a problem, trees down roofs damaged, slight flooding of some land on the estate. Dermot was still living in the cottage with Archie and Colin. He was drinking less saving money, seeing Elizabeth, had met the parents (future in-laws) and sister. It wasn't a warm welcome, more like hell freezing over. Dermot could hardly see himself taking her father out for a pint.

He knew they thought he was a rough mick (they were right). At least he ticked one box – he was a protestant (whatever that was). Her mother was okay with him, he could turn the charm on with her. The sister hated him, there was no love lost between them. She seemed to be seeing some local whose daddy owned a load of local pies, not the baker's variety.

The father was cordial but disapproved at every opportunity, liking to remind him he worked at the estate. Dermot mischievously sometimes liked to remind him of what was going on in Russia. That tended to kill the atmosphere. Dermot played them along, sometimes telling them he intended setting up on his own.

The month before, Dermot had made the local news by winning the Blacksmith Competition at the Royal Highland Show. The Laird was delighted, he'd taken some of his stock up and won a few prizes. The Laird had sent Dermot four cases of stout and a large bottle of whisky, which he and Archie and Colin demolished in one night. Not a lot was done the next day.

The threesome had started getting a reputation. The other workers would land at the cottage for all night affairs, drinking, music, card schools, thankfully the cottage was obscure from the rest of the estate; the gamekeepers had told them to keep the noise down on a few occasions, but had been hauled in and handed a drink.

Dermot tended to see Elizabeth at weekends. It had started innocent but they had gotten more carnal, Dermot babbling to her about setting up on his own. He'd been thinking of it for some time, the work on the estate was drying up, more machinery meant less horses. He seemed to be spending more time fixing gates and railings. He'd taken an interest in the cars, trucks and tractors. He had become quite adept at fixing them. A useful skill, he thought. He saw Elizabeth only at the weekends. He sometimes went in during the week for his dinner, but the atmosphere was always tense and uncomfortable.

He'd heard from Kate. She wrote to him regularly. She'd sent him lots of photos of the baby, James, and the wedding. He looked like a handful.

Kate looked beautiful in her dress. They'd had a small affair. Ken only had one set of living relatives, his brother and family; they had come up from Nottingham. Dermot looked at the photos a lot.

Dermot's mother had started writing to him. He wrote back though not regularly. He told her all about Kate but she never reciprocated. Kate had become taboo. Kate had not heard from her since she'd announced her pregnancy. Kate had effectively washed her hands of her.

His Grandma McNally had died but his mother had said not to bother attending, just his mother and Grandpa left. She never mentioned her brother. Dermot never mentioned him either, dead to both of them, fuck him.

Dermot had been lying in bed. He was waiting for Elizabeth, waiting for sex. He'd been thinking of Emily a bit. Wonder what she was up to, got a vague letter from her at Xmas telling him a lot of boring shite. He'd half read it and put it down. Too much shite about her farm.

Elizabeth arrived in a bit of a state. Fuck, what was wrong here? He was semi-erect. He was wanting to fuck her, not console her. She bubbled away, refusing to speak. Fuck this, he thought.

"I'll get some tea."

He made some tea, the elixir of life. She was still sitting on his bed, patterned summer dress on, hunched up

"What's wrong, Lizzie?"

"I love yeh."

"I know yeh do."

She stood up. She was all for walking out. He grabbed her pushed her back down seated on the bed.

"Whit the fuck is wrong, tell me."

Silence.

"I'm pregnant, expecting a bairn."

Now there was silence, the pair sitting separately for what was minutes but seemed to last a lifetime, Colin shouting his goodbyes from the main room, Dermot shutting his bedroom door. He got closer to her put his arm round her shoulder, she spoke.

"I love yeh."

"I love yeh too."

They held each other. He could feel her salty tears rub against his neck, soft sobs, her hands clawing into his clothes tighter.

"Ma dad'll kill me."

"No he will nae."

The question of abortion was never mentioned. It was face the music time.

"So who knows?"

"No one. The doctor, that's all."

"We'll have to tell my mum and dad, I'm going to see Elsa." Elsa, her best friend.

"I need to git ma head round this."

"Liz, I'll come over to yeh tomorrow night, we can announce it together, okay?"

"Okay… I need to go… I love yeh."

"Liz, I love yeh, just oor plans hae been brought forward dinnae worry."

"I'll see yeh the morn, seven p.m."

She left. She'd come on her bike, he watched her cycle off. It was the end of childhood, welcome to the real world. They were young but there were plenty younger.

He did however think of his options:

1. *Do a midnight flit?*
2. *Ride it out, deny all knowledge?*
3. *Get rid of it?*
4. *Marry and live happily ever after!*

It looked like number 4 was the only option, and in honesty the one he wanted. Colin and Archie arrived back. They knew something was up. He said nothing. They had some beer.

"Whit's up then? Yeh look like someone is dead."

No response. Archie and Colin would have to resort to the heavy brigade. Colin had some cask conditioned whisky they'd acquired; a few hours later the truth had been gotten.

A wedding was all they could think of, yee hah.

"Yeh'll be okay fir cakes."

The bun in the oven joke was going to wear thin.

Dermot was going for the double, no half measures, baby and wedding, up to your knees in shitey nappies. Oh well you never knew what was on the horizon.

Didn't you take precautions? You could get rid of it. For the rest of the night, same questions being asked again and again.

They went and nabbed some sandwiches from the big house kitchen. No one around, help yourself, trouble if you got caught.

Dermot awoke hungover, same clothes, on covered in crumbs. Fuck. He staggered to the toilet, quickly got ready – this was going to be a bad fuck'n day – shouted at the other two, heard the moans.

He got to the smithy on time. He had a team of Clydesdales coming, that'd take care of the majority of the day.

Four p.m. came. The day had cruised by. He was wanting the clock to slow down, his stomach was in knots. He was dreading this. He clocked off, had a beer – he couldn't face food – washed the beer down with some whisky. Threw it all back up and got spruced up. He left before the others got back; he wanted some time on his own. He walked the long walk to the village. It seemed shorter than ever, feeling like the condemned man, guilty plea lodged already.

He went to the local, just nodded at some locals, had three doubles, sucked on a barley sugar to get rid of the smell and went to the prospective outlaws. Should he say 'Hello Dad'? Perhaps not. Or 'You'll look lovely at the Glorious Granny competition, you look so young'? Perhaps not.

The front door was open all of them sitting there, her sister looking like she had a rocket up her arse. Elizabeth spoke, as her father stood up and shut the door

"They know."

Tempted to say 'Know what?'

"I see. Mr & Mrs Miller, I intend to do the right thing here and marry your daughter."

"You're supposed to marry her first, not get her up the duff."

Her sister was dying to chip in.

"Haven't you heard of precautions eh? It'll be the talk of the village."

"And you a tinker and all that."

He'd have liked to have given her a back hander at this point, irritating fuck that she was. There'd be no love with her over the years. She could fuck off with that wet arse she was seeing.

"Well, we'll be getting married."

It now descended into a lecture. Money. Where you staying? Her father was remarkably calm. He said he had a cottage. It needn't some work done to it but they could have it, the sister's face out of joint at this development. Dermot just sat and faced the music. He wasn't really listening. Fuck he wanted out of here. She was three months gone; get the wedding down quickly, didn't want her hobbling down the aisle.

The Wedding Arrangements

And so it went. Dermot sat back and had no say in the matter. It was sorted in four weeks' time on Friday. Marriage in the local church and reception in a local hotel (all paid for and arranged by the outlaws).

Dermot was feeling like a spare prick. He invited his relations (a select few) and some friends, all his mates at the estate to the reception.

The Irish 'mates' contingent did not reply. A few distant relations and his mother said they'd be there, a couple of his old mates wrote saying they'd try (this meant no). Kate couldn't or wouldn't make it due to baby etc. Dermot informed no one from across the water that his bride to be was in the family way (apart from Kate).

Archie and Colin were winding him up no end: babies, shitty nappies etc etc. Dermot had asked Archie to be best man, Colin as usher that was his duties and functions sorted, rings and the suit left.

Dermot was getting pissed off. This was all taking a mind of its own. His father-in-law to be sorting out accommodation for them both and baby to be (the cottage he owned), the mother sorting out the wedding and reception and everything else, dress, catering you name it, only the best for her little girl. He was frogmarched to get a new suit, rings were purchased, all this in four weeks.

Dermot decided he'd fuck off for a long weekend, sorted it with the estate manager. He just packed a bag said he was visiting his sister and was off. Irresponsible was the reply, like he gave a fuck let them get on with it, he needed a break. Two weeks till the wedding...

"Dinnae worry, I'll make it back (ya fuck'n arseholes)."

It was a long journey on the train. Dermot had been to the North of England before, first time to Derby though. He took a couple of bottles of whisky with him.

He arrived late on the Friday night. Ken met him, it was the first time he'd seen him in the flesh but recognised the pictures. They walked back, didn't take long, it was a warm night. They both entered the house. It was nice, all bought and paid for. Ken seemed to have inherited it. Ken was quiet, just gave Dermot the perfunctory chat: how was the trip etcetera, etcetera.

Kate started crying as soon as she saw him. Nearly a year, last time seeing him at the funeral. She looked good, baby was put to bed and supper for Dermot. They'd already eaten.

Kate held him, looking at him. They both smiled. Ken lit a pipe, Dermot a cigarette. Ken produced a couple of bottles of stout and they sat drinking, Ken just making small chat about Derby: the new industries, the factories, what was going on in Derby. They stayed up late into the wee small hours. They even had some of the whisky. Kate just said it as it was, her wedding the baby, how happy they both were. The two of them seemed so laid back, just relaxed. He couldn't imagine himself and Elizabeth like this; they'd also have the interference of the outlaws.

In the morning Dermot heard the baby, saw the baby, cuddled the baby. Uncle Dermot then. He was beautiful, Dermot was in awe. He'd soon have one of his own, the novelty may wear off, Kate said, sleepless nights, dirty nappies etc etc. She was starting to sound like Archie and Colin, put a positive spin on it please.

They had breakfast. Ken had gotten tickets for the football: Derby County playing some other outfit. Derby seemed to have a decent team, some England internationalists.

They went to a local bar. It was filled with the local supporters, everyone getting tanked up before the match. They had a couple, Ken saying you'll never get to a toilet, Dermot not bothered he'd whip it out as and when.

The match was 2–2. It was an exhibition match, some select-side playing Derby County. It was a good-tempered affair, the weather was great, it was a lovely summer's day. They went to the pub afterwards; Ken seemed to be able to hold his drink. He was a good bit older than Kate and Dermot but he was pleasant and funny, his accent amused Dermot, probably vice versa. Dermot couldn't get used to the English ale. They had some stout, which he got stuck into, the whisky was a little pricey but what the fuck he was on holiday.

They got back about six thirty p.m., in time for dinner. It was all ready like clockwork, lamb chops, potatoes and vegetables. Dermot could get used to this. Kate put the baby to bed, Ken did the dishes and cleaned up, Dermot poured himself a drink and sat in front of the fire.

They chatted away, Kate doing all the talking, the men just nodding. Kate just going on about the wedding, Ken's job, how they were hoping to get a car. Ken was signalled to head for bed; he said his good nights and left them. He knew Kate wanted to discuss family matters.

Kate hadn't heard from her mother.

"Are yeh bothered, Kate?"

"Yes and no."

Kate was annoyed. She felt her mother was looking down on her, marrying an Englishman her considerable senior, living in sin, her, a Catholic her mother, a Protestant. She knew her mother's family had never taken to her, whether it was the religion who knew. She thought her mother had been jealous. Kate used to do well at school, why she ended up doing typing secretarial work, how she met Ken. She'd have liked to have gone but it would cause trouble, just tension. Her mother had never been to visit her, never seen Ken nor James. Kate hadn't heard from her since she announced she was pregnant and getting married. She'd sent photos of the wedding, photos of the baby. She'd got him christened in the Catholic Church, she attended every Sunday. She wanted Dermot to come with her tomorrow. Ken never went. He was a heathen, didn't believe in God or nothing. Dermot laughed

"He's heading for hell in a hand cart, Kate. Good for him, he can keep a spot warm for me ha ha!"

"You're terrible."

She press-ganged him into going. Ken was up and off. He had a little patch of garden – they called it an allotment you got it from the council – they'd pop in and see him after Mass. She got the baby ready, got him into his pram. He was all alert, chewing on a dummy. He was all smiles; hopefully they'd all be like that.

The church was as Dermot had remembered. He'd never been an attended to the Protestant faith, forced struggling with his mother to attend (she'd given up on him). Kate had gone on her own to the Catholic Church when a child in Ireland, their father never attending apart from the one offs.

She insisted with speaking with the priest after Mass, attending confession, introducing Dermot to the Father. He was English, not the hard line Celtic type then, fuck that, there was hope for them lot yet. Did he want to do confession? No thank you. Kate telling the priest that Dermot was a Protestant. Oh yes, you mentioned it, Kate, a potential convert here.

They both left with little James. He'd been good as gold. She had some bottles with her, thank fuck for that, he didn't want to see his sister's knockers in the church or street. Some women did that, no fuck'n shame.

They went a walk in the local park. Dermot sat in the swings and Kate placed James on his lap. Dermot went back and forth slowly. James smiled and giggled, biting into his dummy.

Kate was repeating herself, apologising for not coming to the wedding. He told her to stop going on about it. She could come up with Ken and James once they had the car. That would be an adventure for them. Forget their mother, miserable old cunt, he'd have words with her. Wait till she heard Elizabeth was pregnant, the two of them would be tarred and feathered, the shame of it all, her two children both living as sinners.

"C'mon, there's three p.m. We'll have to get Ken."

They arrived at the allotment. Ken had finished what he was doing (if anything) just sitting on a stool with his pipe. Dermot saw Ken was quite the amateur gardener. He seemed to have done quite a lot to it. He even kept pigeons. Kate was going on about getting the dinner ready. Forget it, said Dermot, we can get some fish and chips, my treat.

Ken locked away his stuff, Dermot gave him a hand he padlocked his shed door. They all went down a little lane, Kate manoeuvring the pram to avoid the mud.

They walked back. The nearest chip shop was on the street next to Ken and Kate's so it was a short walk back with three portions of fish and chips for the adults. Kate had stuff prepared for James, he was on a mix of solids and milk. He'd be four to six months old (if Dermot could add). Think she said he'd been born March.

It came the morning of his departure. Ken had said goodbye before he left for work. Dermot, Kate and James walked to the station. Kate cried when he left. Dermot wished he could be closer to her. He'd see her soon enough. She promised they'd visit, that was good enough for him. She'd never let him down before.

Dermot got back about nine p.m. He walked into the town, got a taxi to the village, he couldn't be bothered waiting, took him directly to the cottage. He couldn't be bothered with Elizabeth and her clan yapping about the wedding, she could wait. Archie and Colin were both sitting drinking tea. They poured Dermot a mug.

"How was yir trip?"

"Grand."

"Two weeks tae go then, we'll be having a night out on the Thursday, don't worry we'll arrange it."

"Aye."

Dermot went to bed. Two weeks indeed! Fuck, the condemned man indeed. He thought of Elizabeth's mother. They always say look at the mother, that's what you'll get in twenty years. She looked fine, had been okay with him till he announced he was marrying her and Liz announcing she was up the duff. Some people, no sense of occasion.

So Dermot went to work the next day, for fuck's sake, her father arriving up first thing, think he was checking.

"Just seeing yeh made it back. Got the cottage sorted out, come fir tea the night we can pop over and look at it."

Fuck, this was all change. He'd have to tell the Estate Manager he'd be moving out, more hassle. He seemed to have no control over any aspect of his life, like a lamb to slaughter, probably that fuck'n sister of hers in tow, hopefully without the drip. These cunts would probably be never left the place once the bairn arrived, fuck'n great, stroll on.

The day swept by, he was there at the outlaws, dinner consumed, off to see the house, Elizabeth yapping nonstop, the baby, the house, the wedding. Fuck sake shut it he thought.

Well it was liveable. The cottage was fairly simple, consisting of three rooms and a bathroom, two bedrooms and a living room kitchen. The toilet was an outhouse. A coal fire was always raging in the main room. The fire seemed to control hot water, outside toilet, standards back to normal. That could and would be changed.

"Aye great," said Dermot.

"It comes with a couple of acres of land. You could keep some beasts."

"Aye we could that, could build a smithy as well."

Well it was better than nothing, not like his mother was contributing fuck all. Everything regards his mother would be all in her brother – his uncle's – name. This was all pretty generous.

They went in. Christ, basic furnishings the lot. The garden was all tidy too.

"Got some volunteers to clean up the garden and land."

"Grand."

"We'll let yeh hae a look round. We'll head back."

"Aye."

Dermot and Elizabeth looked around. It was all done out, clean liveable, basic. Dermot was pleased at least with the place, Elizabeth too; she'd be near home. Dermot could cycle in the morning up to the estate.

They walked back to her parents; she was starting to waddle, Dermot had noticed.

"Baby's kicking, yeh wannae feel?"

"Na I'll hae tae get back."

Dermot pecked her on the cheek. Fuck'n arseholes, Dermot thought. He'd been thinking of Kate. Not one of them had asked about her. Fuck'n great, he could predict what the future was going to hold, fuck'n constant interference. Not a one of them asking how Kate, James and Ken were, how was your trip, no just the wedding, the baby, now this fuck'n house more shite to deal with. No America, Australia or…

Dermot went back to the cottage via the pub. He drank on his own, some of the locals congratulating him. For someone getting married he was miserable, he could see his future and it was just a grind: monotony, endless hard labour, a nagging wife, she couldn't shut the fuck up, her mother, her sister.

Aw fuck, he drained another whisky. Why fuck'n him? Too young for this, just his mother coming from Ireland and a couple of his tinker mates, Deck and Brian. Full fuck'n house then, the winning ticket! Christ why me!

The weeks flew in, his mother staying with the outlaws, Deck and Brian staying with Archie and Colin, that'd be some party he knew where he'd like to stay.

The weekend before he had to go to some wedding present display in the afternoon, fuck it he was still going for a kick about in the morning, thoughts of enjoy it while…?

The week sped in, and he wasn't taking anything in really. Kate was sending him a letter a day, the only thing he really looked forward to. He should have gone to Derby when he moved, not here.

The wedding present show was a lip biting experience, her family never admitting she was pregnant, all of the estate knowing as he'd told them. He wasn't ashamed, it happened, fuck them.

Too many old cunts asking him irritating questions, just bluffing his way along. He was getting pissed off with the entire set up, glad when it was over, told them he had an early start tomorrow so had to leave, ending up in the pub till daylight, Archie and Colin nabbing a couple of bottles of the hard stuff from behind the counter before they left.

Breakfast consisted of rum and whisky, Dermot stating that he didn't like rum, but had consumed a half bottle of the stuff. Stop talking shite, they shouted.

They finished the bottles, passed out and woke up mid-afternoon. Archie cracked open some beer.

"Whaur we heading then?"

"Let's gan intae the toon, get the bus, gan a crawl."

"Sounds good tae me."

It was unanimous. The gig was on, no backing out, just mayhem guaranteed. They got all spruced up. Dermot spoke.

"Let's walk in, I want tae avoid the village."

"The outlaws and informers yeh mean."

"The fuck'n arseholes, I mean."

They set off. He could make up some shite story for Elizabeth. The conversation degenerated into two topics: sport and women, Colin and Archie rabbiting on about their latest conquests, half of it a load of shite, sordid imaginations. Archie going on about the Laird's nieces visiting, coming down the garden to see the plants and all, Archie feeling a layer of importance.

"Like they'd be interested in you, ya fuck'n peasant."

Dermot yapping on about football and the internationals, telling them about his trip to see Derby County, how they should get tickets for a big match some time and go, knowing they probably would never get the chance. The cinema had just come in relatively recently, films and all, the talkies were on their way, that'd be grand. What books you reading? Westerns, the unanimous answer.

They hit the first pub they could find, The Royal. They had a pint, The Stags Head and so it went on. Eight pubs later they were in The Cross Keys, a good crowd and still early yet. They'd scoffed some chips, Colin had thrown up.

"Ya fuck'n light weight."

"Making room fir more."

"The night is still young, good sir."

They sat at a table, they were all knackered. Colin had attempted a game of darts, but it was deemed too dangerous, by the rest of the clientele. Archie stood up.

"It is time to call a halt to proceedings, we must retire."

"Shut the fuck up."

But it was true, all legless.

"How are we gettin back?"

"Bus in ten minutes. C'mon, heads up."

Goodbyes were said so it was to be, apart from two police hovering around outside, they were looking for trouble, swinging the truncheons, Dermot of course had to pipe up.

"Evening, *cunt*stable!"

The fact it was said with a venomous Irish accent was all it took.

Dermot had punched one, Archie the other, Colin decided he needed a piss.

"When you got to go!"

Unfortunately there were another few boys in blue on the next street, so now the fun began in earnest. Before they knew it though they were overwhelmed by about six of the bastards. Someone should have remembered the pub named The Blue Lantern down the street was nicknamed the 'boys in blue bar'. Dermot and Archie took some vicious blows. They were cuffed and given a good kicking, Colin marched away.

A night in the cells for the three. Fuck'n great, thought Dermot. In the morning sombre tones, no lip lads said Colin, Dermot tempted to ask what was for breakfast.

"You've got a right shiner, Dermot."

"Tak a look at your face, ya daft cunt."

"It's an improvement."

Colin the only one with not a scratch

"Yeh were a lot of use."

"Law abiding that's all, good sir."

"Shut it."

They got an early bus back in time for a quick change. Thankfully not a date in court, they were off the hook apart from some facial damage, however a note left by Elizabeth. Oh fuck, checking up already, not even married. She'd see him tonight. He was summoned.

Dermot was starting to wish he was still in the cells. He was fixing gates again, fuck'n boredom. He hated it, liked dealing with the horses. The Laird had got himself a Shetland pony. It was the cutest little thing but strong, Dermot was surprised. The Estate Manager came across, congratulated him, told him he'd get the Friday and Monday off, no bother about moving out.

Come to the kitchen on the Thursday at three p.m. They would all have a drink, a presentation on the cards, probable present, Dermot thought. Early day though, then the stag.

So the week raced on at its own pace, it was over. She came over saw his face and left.

"I fell, honest."

Thursday and Stag

Her father volunteered to pick up the three guests from Ireland off the big boat. Dermot's body contribution to the all-day wedding from the Emerald Isle – three. Fuck this was good, you could fit everyone in one car with room to spare. The Scottish contingent for all day – about twelve, all from the estate. Everyone from the estate and village invited to the dance in the local hall, all organised by the outlaws. The agenda was: church wedding, photographs, on to hotel for drinks and meal, on to the dance, all within walking distance. Then back to the new abode, he could carry her over the threshold.

He'd moved out all his stuff to his and hers new abode apart from what he'd need for the next few days, booze and fresh clothes. He had to be at the church for twelve thirty p.m., must be at the church for twelve thirty p.m. MUST.

Dermot had knocked off early and washed and got changed, her father had dumped Deck and Brian at the cottage and went off with his mother back to the village. Thank fuck, Dermot thought, all he needed was an argument with her. Archie and Colin said they'd catch him up at the cottage.

Dermot opened the door to find Deck and Brian already there. They said Dermot's mother hadn't shut up since they'd picked her up that morning. Having to pick her up well in advance (on her orders) they were the first on the boat, they'd gotten a lift to Larne from one of the other lads in a van, she'd been sick all the way over, grand that made him smile.

The pair dumped their bags, producing a couple of bottles a piece of poteen. They all had a few, Archie and Colin arrived making introductions with Deck and Brian. Dermot spoke.

"Get it intae yeh, you lot. Start as we mean to go on!"

"C'mon, let's get this show on the fuck'n road!"

"Fuck ya!"

They set off to the big kitchen, men on a mission. Dermot did the introductions of Deck and Brian, who had their Sunday best on. They would probably have their best on for as long as they stayed.

Dermot's mother was going back on Sunday, whether Deck and Brian made that trip was another matter, once they'd gotten dug in they could be here for a while.

It was 3.20 p.m., the kitchen was full of the majority of staff, at least the ones who knew and liked Dermot. The Estate Manager had had a whip round, cash in an envelope, the Laird had given him an envelope as well (all very generous) so a quick presentation from the Boss and Dermot thanking everyone for contributing and coming, come to the stag night if you so wish, everyone to the night time reception tomorrow night. There was plenty of drink on the go, so they all got stuck in. The head-chef, Charlie, had made up a load of snacks, so a toast was raised to Charlie. A toast was raised to, Dermot and Elizabeth, to Deck and Brian and so it went on...

By seven p.m. they'd made it to the village, more specifically the pub. A good crowd there, all giving him a send-off you'd have thought he'd won the war. Christ Dermot's new father was there.

"Evening, Mr Miller."

"Hello, Dermot, call me John."

"What about Dad, ha ha!"

Deck and Brian were getting the drinks, they got John (Mr Miller) a special drink, spiked to fuck, let's see what he was made of. The fiddlers were playing away, shouting at Dermot to join in.

"Later."

The drink was being downed like it was going out of fashion. Colin had been outside twice to make way for more, Archie singing his head off (badly), John (Mr Miller) consistently reminding Dermot to be there for twelve thirty p.m., telling Dermot how he had to be back home by nine p.m. for the sake of his wife, Elizabeth and Dermot's mother (by this time it was ten thirty p.m., no one was letting on).

"No worries, Dad."

Deck, Brian and Archie had taken to calling him Dad and buying him endless drink, Colin hauling him outside to let him make way for more, Deck telling him,

"You wouldn't want us to take offence about refusing a drink, Dad."

So it was that the old cunt was legless by midnight. Dermot had started playing the accordion, songs were being sung, the doors were locked in the pub, no one was escaping.

Dermot had taken to drinking large 'whisky macs' (whisky and ginger wine accumulated to 100 proof). He was in fine form, they all were. The landlord let the majority out in one go at three a.m., a verbal riot ensued, half singing half shouting, pissing and puking. The villagers heading home, the estate workers heading off to the big house, all though at a slow and noisy pace.

So dad was still there as well, Dermot surprised a search party hadn't been sent out for him, the exercise would do him good.

Dermot decided it was time to go, the remainder of the estates gang all leaving at once, some locals staying (the barman had gone).

They dumped Dad at his doorstep. Fuck this, Dermot thought.

"I think he's pissed himself."

"As long as that's all."

They got back to the cottage about four a.m. Dermot crashed out in Colin's bed. Colin had gone missing, he had a habit of going to the gardens and greenhouse when pissed.

Archie and some of the estate boys sat up drinking till the early hours with Deck and Brian.

Dermot awoke about nine a.m. He checked the main living room. Fire out, standards dropping, he let them sleep. Archie had made it to his room, Deck had made it to Dermot's old room and Brian was sleeping in the chair, Colin missing.

Dermot got himself ready, poured himself a drink, washed shaved, pressed suit on. Flowers to be picked up at church.

Dermot woke Archie, lit a cigarette for them both and went for a stroll, finding Colin in the process, outside sleeping in a deckchair.

The rest went through the painful process of getting ready, not good. One of the chefs had sent over a load of bacon rolls, half abstaining half eating, all of them however drinking.

They all sat outside, round the back of the cottage, a couple of old stools there. Dermot threw up whilst outside. His stomach was in knots.

"Gie me another shot of that poteen."

Dermot knocked into it, he felt like shite, he'd need to get a few more in him. He grabbed the bottle from Brian, slugging into it. Archie gave him a wedding day present, a large hip flask.

"Thanks Archie, it better be full."

It was, of course, with Scotland's finest.

"C'mon lets saddle up."

"You've been reading too many westerns."

"Fuck off!"

So the fun and games commenced, they set off at eleven fifteen a.m., plenty of time, complete with liquid provisions for the long march.

The Wedding

The walk was liquid and fluid. They had a nice day for the wedding, though they were all feeling slightly worse for wear, sunny with the birds cheeping and twittering, but the lads were moaning. They decided to get back on the horse (booze) and all sat on a dyke just outside of and out of sight of the village.

More of the hard stuff was consumed, Dermot sticking to a mix of poteen, cigarettes and a bag of mints. Fuck this, he was thinking, he could have ran a mile (slowly).

The rest of the gang all looked sheepish, time for a motivational chat from Archie.

"Fuck it c'mon you lot it's a fuck'n wedding no a funeral!"

And so it was, the drink was consumed.

They arrived at the Church at twelve fifteen p.m. Dad wasn't there... Yet

"Whaur's Daddy...?"

They waited on the wall, went a walk round the church. Twelve thirty a.m. arrived and eventually Dad arrived with a set of flowers. The minister was there too. Dad was off again, he had to bring the bride, walk her through the village. The kick off was one p.m. and they got themselves sorted. There were people arriving. Dermot didn't know who the fuck they were, just ushered them in smiled a lot, sit where you want.

"Aren't the groom's guests supposed to be on one side the bride's on another?"

"Wha gae's a fuck."

So there was no segregation, everyone piled in, the two mothers arrived together, his one just nodding, fuck'n typical, hadn't seen her in months, not a word.

Dermot could feel the temper rising, could see he'd be having words… later.

The church was about full. He went down the front; the bride would be along shortly. He stood up the front with Archie, Colin, Deck and Brian all winking and giving him the thumbs up. The organist playing in the background. Fuck, thought Dermot, I'm gonna puke, hold it in.

"Yeh got the rings."

"Na I forgot them… I'm joking… relax."

Then the organ started with the Wedding March and it was all stations go. Elizabeth looked stunning. She had a traditional all in white dress, all lace and pattern. Dermot was still trying to hold his stomach in, Archie looked like he was going to pass out, Colin had disappeared outside, Brian and Deck's faces looked like beetroot and they were also suffering from the redeye. Everyone looking fresh, her father was a picture, coughing and spluttering; looked like a Doctor was needed. he might be having a stroke. Oh get on with it he was thinking, this was dragging on.

"I now pronounce you man and wife."

He kissed the bride, she whispered back.

"You stink."

Get the fuck out of here, he marched her out the church, everything hazy. Once outside the recriminations started after being pelted with confetti.

"You lot look like a load of drunks."

"Aye."

"What sort of state was that you brought my father home in? My mother was furious."

"Aye."

"You better behave yourself, this is my special day I don't want it ruined by a load of drunkards."

"Aye."

Dermot's mother of course had to get in on the act, the silent treatment. That was okay though, because he could do without listening to her pish at the moment.

The photographer did his job. Elizabeth was scrubbing Dermot's face with some sort of make-up stuff, get rid of the bruises.

"Aye, aye."

The lads were outside secretly slugging, openly trying to chat up the available girls. The inevitable had to happen: the joint photograph, the two families joining as one. The mongrel was created, Elizabeth's mother yapping at John (Dad) and Dermot, yapping at Dermot for the state of Dad the night before, her telling everyone where to stand, some little kids as the bridesmaids, Archie there in his best man capacity. Dermot wasn't listening to her mum, he had to get the knife into his own mother. He had to say it. He couldn't resist.

"Would have been nice if Kate had been here… James and Ken too."

No response.

"Aye would have been nice if ma only sister Kate could have been here."

Dermot was only warming up, he took his mother to one side and got stuck in.

"So whit's yir problem? I went to see Kate a few weeks ago, yir fuck'n priceless yeh know that she's got a baby YOU'VE never seen."

"Whose fault's that?"

"Shut the fuck up! Yir a fuck'n pious religious shite!

"God the shame EH, EH YA CUNT! Yeh cannae stand it can you, Kate's gone she's happy, living in sin, baby oot off wedlock now married in the fuck'n eyes of God EH! She's got herself somebody that gies a fuck about her and yeh yir jealous. YEH should be happy. But Fuck no not yeh, it disnae suit yeh EH."

Silence.

"Yeh could write couldn't yeh, yeh could visit but that would be fuck'n beyond yeh. Everybody has to run to yeh, is it the religion thing, that's what bothers yeh, it is, isn't it. Yeh made yir bed so you hae to lie in it. Well fuck yeh!"

Still silence.

"I'm surprised yeh even got up of your arse to come to this, where's the rest of them, couldn't be arsed or is it 'The SHAME' eh. The SHAME of it all, child out of wedlock, god sex before marriage, me and Kate yeh must be disappointed. I suppose some cunt relation will be turning in their grave EH!"

"Don't you speak to me like that, I'm your mother."

"Fuck'n act like it then EH! Yeh always have to be centre of attention, the fuck'n Drama Queen. You've made Kate's life a fuck'n misery she feels like she has nae family, only her James and Ken. Fuck it I'll include myself with them. Look at the turnout here, you and a couple of my old friends EH! What the fuck does that say about what YOUR lot think of ME, EH! YOU lot are aw full of shite. The great McNally's the great Daltrey's aw of them full of shite as far as I can see. Not fuck'n one of YOUR lot came to the wedding, at least Deck and Brian made the fuck'n effort EH! Where's your arsehole brother?"

Dermot's mother strode off. Well that was her taken care of, now I can deal with the other old fuck. Dermot was in the mood.

Elizabeth's mother was floating around in the grounds of the church. There were some of hers and Dad's relations there. Dermot had been introduced to them but he could never remember who or what they were to Elizabeth and now him. Fuck the new family.

People were just hanging round now, the main event was the dance at night, but the select few were off to the Hotel for the meal. The photos were done, time to walk to the Hotel, those who were privileged for the meal just family and close friends.

Dermot made sure the lads all got an invite. He'd also checked with the owner that this was going to be no dry affair. It was two thirty p.m. just now as they walked up, the two mothers seeming to get on fine, or was that just Dermot's paranoia? He'd been talking with Dad earlier in the church yard.

"Are yeh okay, Mr Miller? Yeh looked a bit tired last night."

Dad looked around checking no one could hear

"I cannae remember terribly much, all I know is that I woke up outside in the street and Sarah was hitting mae roon the haid, even swearing at me, never seen her like that in a long time, she started hitting me with a dustpan."

So Sarah was Mum's name, 'in a long time', try a couple of decades.

"Well get used to it Mr Miller ha ha!"

"Oh I've been ordered on to soft drinks, I did have an uncontrollable thirst this morning for lemonade."

Dermot thought, fuck'n lemonade, we all had incurable thirst for beer.

"Well yeh'll hae tae hae a drink, the boys'll take offence, and we wouldnae want that now would we?"

"Well I suppose a few but make sure I don't have too many."

"Oh c'mon, Mr Miller, it's yir wee lassie's wedding, should be one of the proudest days in yir life"

Dermot knew that the old git would be legless, he'd make sure of it.

They all entered the Hotel. They had a function room booked. It was the only function room. Some of her relations went and got everyone a drink, her dad had said 'free bar'. This was music to the ears of the lads. Archie was looking as if he was getting there, where he would end up was anyone's guess. As long as he delivered the speech Dermot didn't care.

The function room consisted of two big round tables. They all sat round them; there were name tags, though no one was really bothered apart from Mum (Sarah). The table was all laid out, the full monty, silverware, napkins, the lot, the way it was the times Dermot had seen it at the big house.

So broth for starter, chicken for main, apple crumble and cream, drinks brought through as and when by a couple of waitresses, Dermot and Archie getting the nudge at their table when they insisted on double whiskies.

"I'm only getting married once darling, love and obey remember."

Elizabeth had a face on her, no sex tonight, hadn't been much of that in a long while, think he'd fulfilled his duties, time she did as well.

So tea after the meal, whiskies for the lads. If looks could kill, thought Dermot. They'd even got Dad a doctored drink.

The speeches were quick, thankfully, Archie being staid and responsible just going through the motions, introducing himself.

"I'm the best man and looking around I can see why… blah blah… ha ha."

Dermot gave his speech, just thanking everyone, as did her dad. It was past six p.m. The dance started at seven thirty p.m., though you'd get them arriving at seven p.m. So through to the bar for a few, the women could look after themselves for an hour.

"Still a free bar?"

They were all on the doubles now. Even Elizabeth's relations had joined them, her uncle seemed to be a drinker that was for sure, purple face with veins cracking through. Everyone was puffing away, the women went outside. There was a garden; they seemed to be looking round at the blooms, or at least pretending to.

Archie was getting the doubles poured into everyone including Dad. Dad was looking queasy. Looks like Dads gonnae fall at the next hurdle

"No half measures, folks."

"Cheers!"

"All on Mr Miller."

They took their drinks to the garden. We'd best head over to the dance, Dad was desperate to get going, get the band checked in, make sure the bar was set up by whoever he'd gotten to set it up (some yokels probably) and generally make sure proceedings got underway. Then his tasks were complete, all he had to do then was entertain his highly strung wife.

Archie took control, his last task of the event, not that he'd been hard pushed.

"If we could all make our way from the hotel to the dance."

Deck and Brian wandering across with a glass in each hand, trying to pan drink off on to Dad. Dad was trying to decline politely but the hyenas could smell blood; he was caught in the light.

The Dance and After

So we'd made it, thought Dermot, the worst of it all over, now the dance. The lads piled in. Dermot and Elizabeth stood at the door, because it was summer and because the weather was great the village and estate were there in force. He didn't know who the band were, Dad had hired them to come from Glasgow (no expense spared) so they should know what they were doing.

Archie came to the door and stood with them. He'd brought some drinks. They decided to go a walk round the hall before entering, they could hear the racket from the hall, the music, the screams, the laughter, hopefully marriage would start as this and remain as this.

The three went in. The bride and groom were supposed to kick off the dancing but the crowd had taken charge of events and just decided to do their own thing so dancing had commenced along with drink flowing. Colin, Brian and Deck seemed to be suffering from 'extreme tiredness' or drunkenness and were seated. The place had a sparse amount of tables and chairs; these were commandeered by the old folks.

Dermot and Elizabeth were getting shouted at to dance so they got the floor to themselves, the rest joining in after a short space of time. Dermot didn't even know the name of the tune, some waltz. The band consisted of a drummer, pianist, two accordionists, violinist and even one of them playing guitar. It was quite a combo.

Dermot looked at Elizabeth. She was all smiles and happy but she was tired and moody. Everyone seemed to be enjoying themselves, Dad was getting into the 'spirit' of things. He was being given no choice in the matter.

Dermot was getting grabbed now by Elizabeth's mother to dance, it was dancing and being nagged at in tandem. Archie had hauled up Elizabeth, Brian and Deck seemed to be entertaining his mother (good luck to them). Her mother had started.

"Don't you be getting John drunk tonight."

"Aye."

"John was paralytic last night, a disgrace, couldn't stand up, looked like he'd wet himself so don't you be getting him into that state, he's too old."

"Oh, aye."

"And don't be staying here all night and getting drunk with your pals."

"And get Elizabeth in bed early doors."

"And come and see your mother tomorrow before she goes."

"And let Elizabeth put her feet up, you have to help round the house too you know, you'll have a baby in less than six months."

And so it went on, the dance seemed to last forever.

Eventually Dermot broke free, he sat with Elizabeth she was yawning.

"You want to go?"

"Tell me when you want to go."

She smiled and kissed him, his mother was now trying to make the peace.

"Aren't you going to ask me for a dance?"

Dermot didn't respond just grabbed her and went up, thankfully the tune was nearly finished. Archie had decided it was his time for the limelight and got up and wailed out some noise, fuck knows what. The crowd cheered, they were all up egging him on telling him he was a fuck'n star. He was needing kicked to the moon that was for sure. The crowd were like an organised riot, Archie playing the conductor.

Dermot went to the bar, bought himself a drink. The lads had all paired themselves off with various girls, some locals, some from the estate. Lucky bastards, he'd miss that, now him a responsible married man. He looked at his mother but thought of Kate. He knew she'd be thinking of him, wondered if she knew he was thinking of her.

A couple of the rowdier girls from the estate had hauled up Dad. Dermot watched. It was hilarious, some of the lads egging them on, Archie and Colin standing beside them stomping their feet and clapping their hands, obviously the 'hoolie' was in full swing. Archie and Colin were shouting at Dad now, they had him brainwashed into dancing like a nutcase; he'd be having a stroke at this rate. The band just kept playing faster and faster, everyone was up now. Dermot just sat with Elizabeth watched them all jumping around, it was hilarious

"Can we go?"

"It's only ten p.m."

"I'm very tired."

"Okay let's go."

Dermot and her just slipped out. No announcement, he just winked at Archie, Archie nodded.

They arrived at their home. It felt odd; a few weeks ago all this would have been totally unthinkable, now it had all happened, life speeding by.

He grabbed her at the gate carried her down the path. The front door not locked, in they went. The place was all ready for habitation, they had been working all right. It looked like a home, but it didn't feel like his, everything was hers, now it was all theirs at least in theory.

She went to the bedroom, everything decked out, Dermot hauled up her dress, pushed her doggy style on to the bed.

"Be gentle."

He entered her quickly, he was desperate it had been weeks since the last time they'd done the deed. He grunted as he pumped into her. He slapped her arse cheeks, she moaned back. He was going to come, he groaned but didn't stop; he wanted more. He had her where he wanted her. He started thrusting in hard and deep, she grabbed on to the bed sheets, she was moaning loudly, begging him to be gentle, he wanted it hard and rough. He came again he wanted more he grabbed her hair pushed her into the bed. She moaned at him gently. He came again.

He stripped her off, got her under the covers, took his clothes off and slid under the covers. He put his arm round her. She was tired and all flushed. He played with her, masturbated her until she trembled and orgasmed. He rolled into her and slept.

They woke in the morning. She was tired after the previous day's activities. She ran to the bathroom. She was permanently queasy, he could hear her coughing and vomiting.

It was ten a.m. He'd pop over and see his mother before she left. Dad and Mum were taking her for lunch at midday then to the boat. Brian and Deck would be making their own plans then, doubted she'd be bothered. God knows how she'd get from Larne to home, her problem not his.

So he said his goodbyes to his mother. It was more a grimace with her, things had gone downhill with her in a short space of time, a lot of it down to Kate, but now he had problems and issues of his own with her, let sleeping dogs lie. She could have stayed but she didn't seem to want to and he wasn't asking, unsure of any of her arrangements or travel plans.

John looked out of it. He was pale like a snowman. He'd get the scandal from Archie and Colin, who'd been up to what.

He went back home, it seemed bizarre calling it home but this was it now, ready-made family, life hurtling by, new town, new job, wife, house, and child. So, what next?

Elizabeth was still in bed. Good, he could slip off. He got the bike from the shed, noted that her father had stocked the shed with an array of gardening implements, good man, was starting to like John more by the minute, though it was obvious even to an outsider who wore the trousers over at the baker's. He was destined for an early grave he seemed to be always doing some job for his wife, or Mummy.

Dermot went the long route back to the estate. A cycle ride was what he needed get rid of the cobwebs, her mother would more than likely be over later or vice versa, the weather was still holding. He cycled in to the estate to the cottage.

No smoke, no fire, standards slipping. He knocked on Archie's door.

"Dinnae come in."

Knocked on Colin's door.

"Dinnae come in."

Knocked on his old door Deck replying.

"Dinnae come in."

Oh well at least they were all alive he could hear a lot of giggling, girls' cardigans and hats lying around, naughty boys.

Brian had gone missing. Sure he'd turn up, looking like the boys would be heading back when the money ran out. Dermot had today and tomorrow off, there was no life about so he got a chair took it outside, he could hear some banging, knew what it was tempted to shout out some expletive.

Had a cigarette, grabbed a couple of bottles of beer, Christ it tasted good. He walked up to the kitchen, no one around, there was a table in the hall where any mail was left for the staff. Dermot saw he had a letter from Kate and picked it up. He would have to remember to send her his new address.

He went back. Deck was up, his bit of fluff was gone, she'd been from the village. He couldn't remember her name, romance eh?

Deck handed him a mug, poured it full of poteen. They sat outside both recovering, Deck half sleeping in the sunshine. Dermot was getting hungry. They could get something in the pub. He'd need to get Deck on his feet or he'd be sleeping, the other two could catch up.

"C'mon, Deck, let's go."

He shouted instruction to the gardening duo.

Deck got onto the back of the bike. They were at the pub in a couple of minutes. Deck looked queasy, you'd have thought they'd flown. The pub was empty apart from one drunkard: it was Brian. He was sleeping slumped over a table. Dermot asked the barman when he'd arrived, he was lying outside the bar when I came to open up, was the response. They bought Brian a drink. He moaned. Dermot got some pies.

Well, thought Dermot, it was all go. They sat for hours. Dermot went outside, the other two were sleeping. He went back home. She was up, pottering around. Well, what to do? Well she was going for a lie down. Great, he thought.

He went back to the pub, walked past the in-laws' shop and house, and could see that there was no life. Fuck knows, maybe off visiting. When he arrived back at the pub Archie and Colin had arrived, Archie initiating proceedings the rest not looking too fresh.

Archie gave him the low-down of what had happened after he'd left.

"Basically, Dermot, just loads more drink."

"Dad got a slap from Mum, he was all over the place, threw up outside, the works."

"Myself, Colin and Deck all pulled."

"Everyone else just got leathered, the band got hammered but drove back apparently to Glasgow. They'd be sober by the time they got there."

"And fuck it that was it. Result."

Dermot laughed.

"Glad I missed nothing then."

Dermot and Archie chinked their glasses together.

"Oh well, wha's like us!"

Dermot looked at Brian, Deck and Colin.

"Fuck'n lightweights!"

The pair got stuck in. Dermot got a couple of large whisky macs and off they went on another roll.

The others woke and joined the festivities. They then ended up on the bus

"Wha hey!"

They ended up on a pub-crawl in the toon.

"Wha hey!"

They made it back to the cottage without major incident, apart from Colin falling on his arse when walking along the beach, getting covered in sand and seawater.

"Wha hey!"

Dermot didn't make it back 'home' till six a.m. Not so good.

Fuck, it was the quiet treatment when he awoke, clock saying two p.m., her gone.

Oh happy days, a note on the table. This was the new form of communication then. At the outlaws'. He had a wash, got changed, made himself some food. She'd be back over whenever. He didn't know if he was supposed to chase after her. He picked up a paper, yesterday's local rag, just the usual shite.

He went back to bed after eating some stew. Looked like she'd brought that from her mother's. Hardly see her making something like that.

Woke again, this time it was her it was nine p.m. She climbed in. No sex tonight for Dermot, back to work now, back to normality. This was the new normal. Repetition, repetition. His mother had gone back across the water, disappointed he wasn't there to see her off.

Oh well then.

Back to the Grind

He'd picked up his bike, it was still at the pub. He looked in at the cottage, Brian and Deck still there, sharing his old bed now. Wonder when they'd be off. Soon.

They left and it was back to the fuck'n shite for all.

The weeks and months ground on. Life was like a cycle. He saw less of Archie and Colin. Colin was talking of moving on, Archie telling him he was a cunt if he did. More and more time spent with the new family. The only talk was that of babies, her friends visiting all the time, catalogues with baby clothes, presents from all and sundry for the baby, staying in, saving money, all for the baby.

Archie came across with Maggie. He was having this on off affair with her. She was a bigger nut than him. Colin was homesick, so they hauled him out a few times. His father was ill and he had been close to him in the past.

Kate sent letters. Dermot sent letters and photos of the wedding back. He knew Kate would be happy and sad at the same time. Happy at receiving the photos, sad at not being in them. She'd be coming up at Easter. They'd finalise nearer the time. The baby would be born and she could meet his new family.

Dermot had a visit at the smithy from the Laird. He had a favour to ask Dermot. It always amused Dermot when he heard the Laird had asked a favour. It was if someone would refuse him. He went through the social niceties, could Dermot visit the local Hunt and shoe some horses for them, any money he made he could keep, the Laird just wanted to help the Hunt out. Doubt if any of those cunts had fallen on hard times, thought Dermot.

When Dermot went to the Hunt it was a bigger job than he'd thought. They'd had a part time blacksmith but he'd retired. A lot of Hunt members were professional types. They didn't own any land as such but paid the Hunt to look after a horse for them.

Dermot went over at nights for an entire week. He worked about another five hours every night. The money did help.

The Head of the Hunt was a bit of an old duffer but he had a sense of humour and kept Dermot fed and watered, and paid well too. It was a new experience and lesson for Dermot. He could go it alone and drum up business. The Huntsman told him there was a real shortage for someone of Dermot's talents.

It was something for the future Dermot thought.

Blues

Dermot had never been religious. He'd seen enough of 'my god is better than yours' brigade, Dermot and Kate the product of the volatile love of humanity's relationship with The Lord Almighty.

What was about to happen would perhaps change all that, from a dislike of God and his Works to Hatred.

The night before the event was nothing spectacular, just came back home on the bike had a cup of tea with the lads and set off from the estate.

Got back, she wasn't there, note on the table. Food there or come to her mum's. She was feeling sick and had been for the last month. The doctor had given her some medicine but just put it down to her pregnancy. He was tired, couldn't be bothered going across but did so after he'd eaten, she was sleeping and in bed so he didn't wait. She'd stay the night there.

In the morning he went the bike ride to the estate as usual, started the fire and went about his routine and job.

Dad arrived at the Smithy. He'd need to come with him, he'd told the Estate Manager, Dermot went via the gardens but Archie and Colin were nowhere in sight. Dad had the car

"Whit's wrong?"

"I dinnae know the doctors there though."

So it was, the doctor was in the hall, took Dermot outside.

"I'm afraid the child is dead."

Dermot was stunned.

"It was a girl.

"I'm afraid Elizabeth's had a miscarriage, she's lost the baby. I'm afraid it wasn't to be, son."

Dermot went to Elizabeth's bedroom, her sister there crying, Elizabeth just doped but conscious, just mumbling. Dermot wrapped his arms round her for what seemed like a long time. The rain had started. It was apt. It rattled against the window. Her sister left the room, Elizabeth cried and cried and she cried. She was blaming herself, Dermot whispering at her.

"Sssshhhhh."

She slept. He climbed on to the bed with her. They gave her more medicine. She had lost a lot of blood but would recover. It was ten p.m. Dermot should go home. They'd inform the doctor who'd informed the estate saying he wouldn't be in. Her mother told him to go home, he was no use to her making himself sick, he nodded and left. Her father gave him a bag of assortments from the bakers.

"Go rest, son."

He walked back. He could see lights on in the other houses life going on, people going about their business. Everyone in the village would know soon enough, then it would be crying, tea and sympathy, everyone saying how sorry they were, could they help in any way, aye they could fuck off.

He climbed into bed. The matrimonial bed, their bed. Her mum and dad had bought it brand new.

He had a letter from Kate. It had been delivered this morning. He opened it. Kate was just telling him the same old same old. She'd enclosed some photos, the three of them together how a family should be. He lay awake for what seemed like an age, had a couple of cigarettes, dumped the ash on the floor, got out of bed, and sat in a chair beside the fire, which was out. He rekindled it and fell asleep.

Morning came. He had a wash and went to see her. She was sleeping, she needed rest. Her sister sat with her, Dermot sat with her father in the living room, the baker's shut. The village would know, the estate would know. News spread fast. Some of her friends came by. They went in and sat with her, all the women together, all the men together, the men making small talk. There would be no funeral. The doctor took care of everything. It wasn't to be. God had decided.

Archie arrived across at night. He'd brought flowers. They got up and left went for a walk. Archie wanted to take him to the pub, Dermot said let's just go back to mine. They both sat at the table. Dermot had drink left over from the wedding. The wedding seemed like an eternity ago. Archie telling him, like everybody else, you have plenty of time for kids.

After a few days Elizabeth came home. Her mother and sister were never far from sight. Dermot returned to work, glad to get back, back into the swing of things, get back into a routine, back to normal.

Dermot and Elizabeth got back to normal but it was if they were leading separate lives, the reason they had gotten together was gone.

"We can try for other children."

The sex was mundane and lifeless. They both kept making excuses not to do it. This soon became the norm. They both lived separate lives. Unfortunately love was turning to hate. She consistently ignored him and they never spent time together, always doing other things, alterations to the house, bathroom, toilet etcetera, just to do something else.

The Easter Visit of 1922

The visit had been talked of but finally came about. Ken, Kate and James arrived in a little car. Dermot was excited about them visiting. He could have invited his mother across but that would have resulted in friction; his mother had taken to writing to Elizabeth which suited him fine. He couldn't be bothered with dealing with her at the moment and Elizabeth seemed to enjoy relaying her news of Ireland to him. Elizabeth was under instruction not to tell his mother that Kate was arriving. That would be like the red rag waved at the bull.

Kate had written a lot to him. It helped. He knew she cared and that was all he needed at this time, someone he could rely on, a shoulder to cry on.

They arrived and were staying for a week, they could stay in the spare bedroom. It was all set up. No one had stayed in it apart from Archie or Colin after one too many on a cold night.

He hadn't seen Kate since before the wedding. It had taken them the best part of the day to get there. The three were tired. Because Elizabeth didn't know when they were arriving she'd just made loads of sandwiches.

They all sat round the table, idle chat. Ken looked tired, a long drive, Kate was learning to drive under Ken's insistence. The baby was sleeping. Kate put it in the spare room; they had a cot with them. He was at the age he couldn't walk but could crawl, said Kate.

They sat for a while longer just drinking tea. Dermot had taken the end of the week off, but would have to go in for the next couple of days. They'd all have to entertain themselves.

Dermot got up earlier than usual. He could knock off early. He sneaked around and left, trying not to wake anyone, cycling the usual route, past the cottage, good memories there with Archie and Colin.

Colin had moved back up north. He'd been offered a job nearer to his family. Archie had been pissed off with him, but they gave him a good send off.

Archie had two new men in the cottage. One was a young lad called Davie from the Borders – he'd taken over from Colin – and a fellow called Graham who was an addition to the gamekeepers, but Graham was leaving in the next few weeks, heading to the city, he kept saying.

He'd pop over and see Archie, tell him Kate was here. They could have a night out or in, probably both. They could take Ken down the pub. That would be an education for him. Dermot's accordion was still in the pub, it hadn't even graced his new home.

Dermot got on with his routine. He could see Archie and Davie. They were going round the estate, they always seemed to be pottering at something, skiving would be another term, though Dermot had to admit the gardens always looked spotless and beautiful all seasons. Elizabeth always liked when Archie came across. He always brought plants and flowers. He'd come across and helped Dermot out doing the garden, converting the land. They'd even bought a couple of sheep and some hens. Dermot would never have turned the land round as Archie said to him.

"Yeh may have hands of steel, you don't have green fingers."

Midday, time for a break. He'd taken the leftovers from the night before, and there they all were, they had come across. Hang around I'll get Archie. Archie and Davie made their introductions, Kate spoke to Archie.

"You're Archie, I've heard all about you."

"Only the good I hope."

Ken had lit up his pipe Dermot got a light.

"We're going into town for a spot of something to eat."

Kate was clinging on to the baby and Elizabeth was in awe. Dermot wasn't sure if this was a good thing. They told him they'd stopped in for the morning at her parents'. Good, thought Dermot, that's that out of the way. He pecked Elizabeth on the cheek, told her he loved her. Archie spoke.

"Aw right for some. C'mon Davie, we'd better get back, nice to meet yis we'll see yeh aw afore yeh go."

"Dermot, we'll crack on we'll see yeh later."

"I'll be back early."

When they'd gone Dermot went over, told them to come over tomorrow night for their dinner. Bring Graham as well.

"I'm going to take Ken to the pub tonight if you're up for it."

"Thought you'd never ask. We'll have to show the English some Scottish hospitality."

Fuck, thought Dermot, probably half of them had never seen an Englishman.

Dermot headed back home. The weather was holding. When he got back he saw Ken's car, so they were back.

"How was the meal, where'd you go?"

They told him where they'd been what they'd had…fish

"How's James?"

"He's fine."

Elizabeth was cradling him, Dermot was glad to see her smile. It's a shame none of Elizabeth's friends had children, it might do her good. She should get involved with the local nursery, get the fuck out of the baker's.

Dinner was going to be a fry up, no complaints from anyone. Dermot went for a wash and they all sat down. Kate had James off the milk (thankfully no breast incidents). He was on some type of baby food.

Once they'd eaten, Dermot and Ken went outside and smoked. Kate and Elizabeth cleaned up and came out. They all sat on some chairs Dermot had 'acquired' from the estate; he'd be 'acquiring' a table at some stage as well.

"I'm taking Ken down the pub tonight. He can meet some of the lads."

"Oh are you now! We don't get an invite then?"

"Yeh wouldnae like it."

"Help yirself, yeh know where they are. Keep the noise down. Graham's still in his bed"

Dermot opened a bottle of stout.

"Cheers."

They finished the beers, walked to the car and Ken drove them back.

"Ken, stop at the pub, I'll pick up the accordion."

The accordion was picked up, sarcastic remarks from the bar staff and clientele as to the state they were all in last night.

"That was just a warm-up for tonight, we're in training."

They all trooped back to the house, Kate, Elizabeth and James sitting in the garden, Archie with the obligatory bunch of flowers. Dermot went and had a wash, by the time he came back they were all sitting drinking.

"Something smells good."

The dinner was cooking away, chicken and trimmings, some cake and cream from the baker's for dessert.

They went inside, the table all laid out, well the girls had done a good job. James fed and packed off to bed.

They all finished, drinks flowing. Dermot was going to start the accordion, the girls spoke in unison.

"No the Bairn!"

No shouting, singing or music tonight then, they sat and told stories. Ken was rambling on he seemed to be enjoying himself. So was Dermot, so was Elizabeth, they all were; this was what life was supposed to be all about, the good things in life, not the heartache, and they'd had enough of that of late.

Dermot had the end of the week off but the days flew by, Elizabeth becoming more and more bonded to James. Dermot and Ken getting on fine, they went on an all-day fly-fishing trip. Dermot caught nothing, Ken caught two brown trout.

"Beginner's luck."

Kate and Elizabeth spent a lot of time together, they'd hit it off thank Christ. They all went in Ken's car to visit a local religious site called St Ninians Cave. It was a cave this monk Ninian was alleged to have lived in. He'd brought Christianity to Scotland back in the day. Dermot and Ken looked at each other. Dermot had never been, Elizabeth had. Dermot felt like saying not much of a fuck'n cave. Ken was looking like he might laugh, Kate was doing all that praying stuff. Oh well. Good for her. Dermot piped up

"Fascinating then."

Ken was thankfully looking away. They trooped off. There were lots of little sites around historical ruins, they spent the rest of the day visiting them. They went to the Galloway Mull. You could see Ireland and the Isle of Man from there; you could see the Isle of Arran and the Ailsa Craig (a redundant volcano) from the toon. So they covered all the tourist sites, had a day in the toon, buying James some toys in the local stores, going for lunch, going for dinner, a holiday at home for all.

Dermot eventually got time on his own with Kate. Elizabeth was dealing with James, Ken had spotted a fancy little tobacconists. He vanished indoors.

Kate hadn't heard from their mother

"She hates me."

"Oh fuck her, look she's jist difficult, look I've had limited contact with her, Elizabeth and her write but there's nae news it's just a load of awld shite, the same old, same old, stop worrying about her or thinking about her."

"She's my mother too, I think she always resented me, she's supposed to love me the way I love James. You know I was conceived out of wedlock, then James oh yes she likes to remind me."

Dermot knew he could say or do nothing to change the state of affairs, he just wrapped his arms round her, told her he cared and loved her, she had a lovely son and good man, thank your blessings, he told Kate he hadn't seen Elizabeth as happy or lively in a long time.

Ken appeared back. He'd bought half the shop, thought Dermot. He handed Dermot a big packet of cigars and some rolling tobacco.

"Here's something for you," said Ken.

"Yeh shouldnae bothered that's grand."

"No problem."

Dermot thanked him and they all headed back home. They bought some fish and chips, they could stick them in the oven if they got cold.

They sat and played some cards, it'd been a while since Dermot had played, it whiled away the hours, all of them knowing the last night was the worst. We'll come to Derby end of summer, Elizabeth nodding.

The visit had rekindled something in the two of them, perhaps things were on the up.

1921-1928

After Kate left things were fine between Dermot and Elizabeth. Dermot asked to cut down his hours at the estate and built himself a smithy at home, they had the space and land. Dermot got the lads in and it was built over a weekend. Dermot had broadened his business horizons, there was work there for other farmers but if the estate needed things done he was there; it suited the estate as he was doing the same job except doing it part time. Dermot worked for local businesses, farmers, horse owners, anything to do with metal he was your man. He had gotten himself a new van with his name and profession down the side of it.

At home they got on better, Elizabeth working at the baker's as and when, Dermot doing his thing however they were drifting apart. They didn't tend to spend too much time together. Dermot stayed away when he started taking jobs further afield, still socialising with the lads and at times acting as if he was single. The Irish Wild Rover was still alive and kicking. After Kate had gone he had gone back to the Royal Highland Show, got a second this time, but seemed to end up on the drink for a week, popping in to visit Colin up north in the process.

He'd decided to enter a competition back on the Emerald Isle, The Royal Ulster Show. Dermot had been in it years ago, had done okay. This time he had a reputation though. This time however it was a disaster: arrested thrown in jail, thumped a few people at the show, it would be a doubt if he got asked back or would want to go back.

Whilst across he'd visited his mother. It was a tense affair. He'd got notice a week after they'd buried her father about a month previously, obviously he was superfluous to requirements. It didn't go well. He left after one night. She was dead to him. He'd never know why she seemed to resent himself and Kate. It saddened him initially but the older he got it just angered him.

On the baby front they were trying again but to no success. Dermot kept telling her to relax it would happen soon enough, enjoy the time they had together. Elizabeth had kept a lot of the baby stuff, but it was housed at her parents'. Elizabeth thought that Dermot didn't know, but he did, he let it pass and never mentioned it, let sleeping dogs and all that.

They had arranged to go in September to see Kate. They were all set; Dermot could drive the van down. Dermot found the journey a trek, could see it couldn't have been much fun for Kate and Ken with a baby in tow. When they arrived it was as if it was yesterday, as if it had been last week. Elizabeth had loaded the car with presents, Dermot with whisky. He'd been and gotten Ken some of the fancy tobacco and cigars he'd had in Scotland.

Elizabeth made a beeline for James, Dermot for Kate and Ken puffed his pipe and poured the drinks after they'd emptied the van.

"You moving to Derby then?"

Dermot laughed.

"Aye I liked it that much the last time ha ha!"

"Fish and chips tonight, the housewives' favourite."

"Fish and chips every night."

Ken went out and got them all a round of the housewives' favourite, he walked back puffing away; the rest stayed at the house, unpacked and spoiled the baby Mr James.

They ate the food. Elizabeth had brought a load of cakes and stuff from the bakery. Ken was just telling them about what was happening, he and Dermot arguing politics. Ken a labour man, Dermot just a paid up member of the Argumentative Party. We can go to the pictures tomorrow, we can get a babysitter. The days went in quickly; the cinema, the shops, the football, County winning 4–3, the local pub, Dermot meeting some lads he'd met in the same bar the last time he was there.

Time to go came round quickly. Kate had been pressing them on the baby question, Dermot pressing her on their mother and the deceased grandfather, nothing resolved. A load of tears were shed, it was a sad journey home. They both liked Derby. Dermot started on Elizabeth, he thought he'd see the lie of the land remarks such as plenty of work, opportunities, better standard of living. It went in one ear, out the other.

Back to Scotland, Galloway, the village, it was home…for now.

Over the years he and Kate kept in touch his mother remained silent. They tried for a baby but over the years it resulted in tears. Elizabeth had miscarriage after miscarriage, it was heart-breaking for her but soul destroying for Dermot. No one ever mentioned it but everyone knew, they stopped after her third telling anyone it was their business, they'd deal with it. Dermot couldn't stand her moods and did what he could to stay out of Elizabeth's way. It was tears, tantrums and arguments, non-stop bickering. Dermot's moods were getting worse. He'd smash things up, started taking it out on others, arrested on numerous occasions, the police reluctant to get involved with him, Archie bailing him out frequently. A local policeman gave him his last warnings, no more or it's jail. He stayed in more and more, stayed away from regular pubs but drinking more and more, arguing more and more with Elizabeth. His work was starting to get affected, jobs cancelled, jobs botched. Dermot was a freight train out of control with no brakes.

It was autumn 1926. He'd been drinking all day, had been out for a walk, couldn't be bothered doing much and left Elizabeth to it. Now they'd started keeping animals Elizabeth did the majority of the work in this respect, keeping cows for milk, a couple of sheep, and fuck'n hens making noise all day. Those fuckers were close to getting the chop.

His mother had died the year earlier, no word till after she'd been dead and buried. Her arsehole brother keeping control of everything. Dermot had consulted a solicitor. Everything had been in arsehole's name all along for years. Her mother dying the year previously, he'd weaselled in, fuck him he was welcome to it. All contact with Ireland ended. The worst was informing Kate. He'd got word to her, she was in a state, nothing anyone could do now. Nothing remained of any sentiment, no photographs, nothing. It was if the two didn't exist. Uncle Arsehole could fuck off.

He staggered in. It was dark, chickens in their coop, thank fuck they shut up when it was dark. He kicked the door open, food on the table, no sign of her, she'd be at her mother's. He ate his dinner, fell asleep in the chair. He woke hearing her coming back, a load of lip from her, everything his fault, babies, drinking, work, money… and he snapped.

He pinned her down one hand wrapped round her throat, telling her to shut the fuck up. He struck her twice then couldn't stop, losing count. She had work trousers on, he tore them off. He raped her repeatedly, shouting abuse at her, not punching her slapping her, telling her to shut up, telling her to start treating him with some respect. Her lip was swollen, her face was swollen. Her face would be black and blue in the morning. She shuffled to the bedroom like a wounded animal. He pulled his trousers up, sat on a seat shouting abuse through the door, bitch this bitch that.

Her first thoughts were what she'd look like the next day – what would people think, her parents, her sister, her friends. All she could hear was his cursing, ranting and raving, shouting abuse, things getting thrown around, a lunatic on the loose. Her thoughts turned to herself; it was her fault, her moods, she blamed him too much it was her fault. He screamed and shouted then he left, she heard the door slamming nearly off its hinges.

She lay awake for ages, thinking of all the things she'd have to do, the animals, other chores. At least she'd stopped the baker's, too much to do here.

She was awake. Oh no, the animals, she went to the kitchen, it was all tidy; she went to the barn all the animals were out in the field, the chickens fed, the sheep could look after themselves.

She could hear him pottering in the smithy, he'd changed into overalls.

"Go back inside. Go to your bed."

No apology, no acknowledgement. She was exhausted. She went to bed, she slept all day. She looked in the mirror. One of her teeth was missing, she couldn't even remember, her face was a mess, she cried on the bed, listening to him hammering away.

She got up, peeled some potatoes, there were tins of meat there that would have to do. He came in washed ate what she'd prepared and left. No response, nothing.

This became the norm, it reached the point she couldn't hide it, you can only tell the lie so many times, I fell, teeth don't just fall out.

To him it was if nothing had happened. He seemed to have spells of abstinence then it was the devil returning, his moods. He never said sorry, never acknowledged any of it, it was repetition. She learned to avoid him when his dark moods came down. Everyone knew but no one ever said, what happened behind closed doors was their affair. Archie though did speak, he acknowledged it to Archie even said he was sorry what he was doing but he never stopped doing it.

It therefore came to pass what became normal; everyone knew but no one spoke out. Archie tried and failed, friends didn't visit as often, she visited her parents and sister more. Her sister had got married but they never visited, Elizabeth sometimes went and visited her. Dermot never raised the issue. He sometimes popped into her parents but it was brief. Archie had gotten married to one of the girls from the estate, he'd moved from being a gardener to taking over one of the tenant farms, more money, Davie filling his boots in the garden. Dermot visited Archie but their infamous nights out were rare, the responsibility of the farm taking up much of his time. Dermot went to the bar drinking on his own more and more, the solitary drinker.

He came up with the idea of a band, the fiddlers were up for it. They got the hold of a few others, Dermot took charge and bought a van, they had a load of bookings all over. Dermot took it seriously, bookings months in advance, big money. They were all doing it as a hobby but it was a big money earner for them all. It also meant more time away, less time for hard work, less time dealing with Elizabeth.

Her father died. It was all sudden, she was devastated. At least he loved her. Her mother was devastated and her sister. Dermot felt nothing. He'd been a good man, he'd set Elizabeth and Dermot up in a house, they couldn't complain. He felt no pain, a heart attack, good turnout at the funeral, flowers, telegrams and cards from all over. Archie attended, the pair had a good drink, going over nights out, the good old days, promising each other to meet up sooner rather than later, come and see the band, come and see the baby when it's born, due in a few months, the conversation quickly turned to another subject, so it was.

Dermot's business plodded away. He made enough to get along on, enjoying the band most. Elizabeth soldiered along with the animals, house and helping her mother. Her mother kept the baker's going, her sister helped when she could. She'd given birth to a little baby girl, it was named Elizabeth too. Elizabeth was made up, Auntie Liz, Dermot never bothered, he had no time for her.

The years passed no one got any younger, they still had sex no result was forthcoming, the beatings happened, the drunkenness happened. Happiness for both was non-existent.

Babies Arrive and Old Departures

Elizabeth took matters into her own hand,s put her foot down, attended a specialist, a gynaecologist, 'women's trouble'. It worked. She was pregnant again. It had just turned January 1929, she hadn't been pregnant for three years. Dermot had given up. He had sex to relieve himself; there was no real love between them. It was just an act. Dermot had become rougher and she was only there for a purpose. She moved in with her mother for three months, claiming her mother was ill, the truth being she wanted him nowhere near her. Dermot hadn't seen her in a while she was now four months gone, she knew he suspected so she told him, he got drunk… he then didn't drink for months.

She gave birth to a boy, she called him Jimmie. It was October 1929.

She gave birth in the local hospital. Everything went according to plan, her mother and sister attending, Dermot waiting outside till the birth, then arriving at Archie's that night to 'wet' the baby's head. Archie himself had become a dad recently so the two were comparing notes. It had been a smooth birth, there perhaps was some justice in the world for Elizabeth.

Before the birth she had everything prepared: the spare room was sorted, toys were purchased, clothes were plentiful, everyone and sundry buying the baby something, the baby was an attraction.

Dermot was pleased the prodigal father had delivered.

About a year after the birth her mother died. It was a shock as Elizabeth again was pregnant, everyone was worried for her.

Her mother had just died in her sleep. It was one of those things, there was no warning whatsoever. The funeral, again well attended, the village community coming together.

The baker's business went to her sister, Elizabeth had after all received the house she and Dermot lived in, though of course Dermot didn't see it this way, biting his lip, letting loose to everyone and sundry when drunk.

"She never liked me."

Elizabeth again gave birth, again a smooth birth, this time to a frail little girl. She was born in September 1930, Audrey.

Kate came up with James on both occasions. Ken couldn't make it, promotion at work, she came by train, James a little man now, the countryside a great adventure. He spent the majority of his time with Uncle Dermot, working with the animals, watching Uncle Dermot with the horses, Dermot taking him fishing, teaching him boxing at nights. James amazed at all the wild animals around, wild rabbits everywhere.

Kate had laid into Dermot when she got him on his own, told him to behave himself, he had responsibilities now, major responsibilities, start behaving like a grown man. It worked, at least for a while.

5
1945–1960

The war had ended. It had been a major global event, a lot of young local men did not return, the POW camps were still in operation, it would take time for these men to return home. Some decided to remain. Families in the area had lost many, families all over had suffered and would continue to suffer. James had died in the household but other friends had been lost; Archie had lost his younger brother. The loss had taken it out of Ken and the end of the war reinforced it. Ken never mentioned it but he'd been through the 'Great War' and knew what the returnees were feeling, friends lost forever but never forgotten.

Jimmie had left school just after he was fourteen years old, been taken under the wing of his father to learn the trade of blacksmith. Dermot was not the most temperate nor best teacher around. Jimmie survived the moods, the beatings, it just became the norm. Dermot left the hard work to Jimmie.

Jimmie was not physically built like his father. He did not have his father's size, if his father was a heavyweight he was certainly a flyweight. Dermot was hard to please, Jimmie found out early on that nothing was ever to his father's pleasing.

By 1950 Jimmie was effectively running the business. Dermot had become introverted, he seemed to spend his time drinking.

The abuse of himself, his mother and sister had toned down in the last few years. Things had come to a head as regards his sister in the years before. Enough was enough. The fact that Jimmie was no longer putting up with it physically or mentally also was a significant factor. Dermot didn't seem to have the fight or energy to argue anymore. He was bothered with bronchial trouble, cigarettes didn't help nor did heavy manual work or excessive drinking, but Dermot liked to try. Dermot spent more and more of his time with Audrey, with the band. This suited him to a tee, late nights, music. In Audrey's eyes as the years went on he became more hindrance than help; she loved and hated him in equal measure.

Jimmie had built up good relations with the new Laird. The old one had died and his nephew had inherited it all. He seemed like an amiable 'toff' as Jimmie liked to call him, but Jimmie had secured a lot of business with the Laird. Jimmie had broadened his horizons and had got contracts with the local council: gates, railings, welding, anything to do with metal. He tried his hand at the competitions for blacksmithing and won his fair share. He had to pack it in for a couple of years and Dermot had to do it for him, the master returns. The reason was simple: National Service. Everyone had to do it. He had been drafted into the local Infantry Regiment. Jimmie hated it. He had inherited his father's disrespect for authority, he had also picked up his father's talents for drinking and smoking, something he seemed to show a natural aptitude. He had unfortunately picked up his father's talent for violence. This got him into trouble in the Army on numerous occasions, sometimes he got off thanks to his C/O being a boxing fan.

Jimmie was a natural and represented the Regiment. Jimmie was a contradiction in terms though as he had also become quite religious in the Army, regularly attending church services, bible at his bedside. His comrades thought it bizarre, as he was regularly the life and soul of the party and certainly had no inkling or desire to be abstinent. His time in the Army was slow, spending the majority of his time in the North of England.

He came back when he could and caught up with his mother and sister, his letter writing perhaps not up to scratch or perfunctory. Oh how he hated military structure, orders, marching, the Army owned you, all of you.

Audrey had effectively taken over the day to day running of the band with bookings during the week, regular venues and one offs, a whole array of new venues. The war was over, people wanted to forget, they wanted to party. Audrey had become known nationally through chance, she had been to Norway on an exchange visit after the War and it had been mentioned whilst in Norway the little Scottish girl could play the accordion. Before she knew it she was playing on Norwegian National Radio, this of course got back to Scotland. She ended up on local Scottish Radio and this helped gain bookings. She was famous in a little way. As an extra form of income she had taken to teaching. This again was good business, as the area became an accordion hotbed and the love of this type of music spread.

The years after the war had been rough for Audrey. Her father had taken his sexual attentions to herself full-time, always when drunk, he'd beat the other two, then rape her. The consequences were inevitable: miscarriages, the local doctor suspicious as to what was going on. It culminated in an illegal abortion for Audrey that nearly killed her. It would affect her physically and mentally the rest of her days.

She had to go away after this and went to stay with Kate and Ken for a time. Kate kept it to herself, Ken knew nothing. The story was Audrey had blood problems, the break would do her good, she could put her feet up etc.

The death of James had taken it out of Ken and Kate. Ken bottled it up, Kate spent more time at church, Ken at his allotment. The two were shells of themselves, they went through the motions of life they drifted apart but they still deeply loved each other. Anyone could see this but dealing with the tragedy had been hard. They knew other parents who had lost loved ones, there seemed to be loss everywhere. Derby had suffered, as had they.

In 1951 Ken died. He was older than Kate. Kate died the following year she was only fifty-six years old, it could be said they both died of broken hearts. Dermot, Elizabeth and Audrey went down and arranged things. Ken still had a surviving brother. He travelled up from down south and helped the trio; they went through personal effects, it was harrowing for all as there were photograph albums filled with James but also photos of Kate and Dermot growing up. The wills were split amicably.

Dermot was devastated, they had always been close, his sister had always stood by him no matter what. She had tried in later years to get him attending church, convert to Catholicism, anything to get him on the straight and narrow. She seemed to be able to get through to him more than anyone else but it was usually short lived and once she was gone or her influence was removed he returned to his old ways. The journey there had been

parents, the landlord a friend of theirs, his brother working there after leaving the Army, his brother seemed to have a knack in the bar trade.

The families were all 'tea and cakes', Ted and Audrey glad to get everyone going on their way. Ted off back to his unit tomorrow, taking Audrey out for a meal before he left, Audrey delighted to wave her engagement ring around. Audrey had noted that Ted and his brothers all got on fine but there seemed to be no love lost between all of them and their father.

So it all passed. The wedding took place in the Easter, all attended and everyone had a good time.

The following year Elizabeth was found by Dermot in the chair he liked to frequent. She had died young, too young. Life had been a mixture of good and bad times in unequal measure. Her sister and the remnants of her family attended, Dermot, Jimmie and Audrey shocked. Dermot took it bad. He felt guilt and so he should. Jimmie was upset but life went on. Audrey had been living on her own in the flat but she spent her spare time at her parents'. She moved in for a while with her father, but she moved back to the flat, she never fully trusted Dermot nor ever would.

Nine months later Dermot died. He'd gone downhill quickly once Elizabeth had gone. He was full of regret, bitterness and self-pity, where had all the dreams gone, America the New World, travel, all too late.

Audrey looked after him. She sometimes stayed. She was less scared of him in his final months, he was just a frail weak man. He had been ill for some time, not just on a physical side. Lunacy had run in his family.

He'd been getting forgetful, argumentative asking for Kate, Elizabeth and Archie. Kate and Elizabeth were dead. Archie would visit and sometimes would receive no acknowledgement.

Dermot was confused and frustrated, not recognising those closest to him nor remembering the past or the present. He suffered from extreme memory loss, waking not knowing where he was, who he was, what in general was going on around him. He would eat a meal then eat another forgetting he'd just had one, he'd go walks and get lost. Archie would be in tears when he left visiting him. Dermot would sit dreaming of the westerns and America, John Wayne, Randolph Scott, boy he loved it all, he was there.

"It happens to us all."

His funeral was well attended, Archie there as always, Colin came down from north. The pair said their final farewells to the 'Mad Irishman'. Accordion music was played into the early hours. Dermot was off to the Great Western.

Audrey thought of her mother, Jimmie thought of his mother. He was gone for good, a new era, everything split down the middle.

6
Ted

Ted was born in 1937 to John and Gwen. She was a maid on an estate, he a gamekeeper. He had two elder brothers, Keith and Dougie. They were all kids during the war, none old enough to fight. The war really meant nothing to them. POWs working on the field, servicemen training in the area, naval and air activity going on. Rationing meant nothing to all of them; you didn't miss what you'd never had. They lived in a ramshackle cottage which was extremely isolated; others called them 'the hillbillies'. It was remote.

The three sons spent their time doing what children do or at least trying. The father was strict and abusive, and the mother was just strict but scared and cowed. It was like existing in a military regime. Religion paid a part, the Kirk was visited every Sunday, the father had the bible in one hand, the belt and bottle in the other.

Ted's mother and father had a loveless relationship, no one knew why they had gotten together. He had no surviving family, she had two sisters. Ted adored one of them, his Auntie Jenny. He was named after her husband Eddie (Edward Curran). The other one, Mattie, lived in town. The contrast between the three sisters was marked. Mattie was a party girl, Jenny was outgoing and lively, Gwen who knew. She had changed into a Presbyterian lifestyle. This was to be led by all.

Eddie and Jenny lived nearby. Eddie worked on another estate but kept a lot of land of his own which he spent all his time working on. Jenny couldn't have children, so Ted was the surrogate son.

Ted spent his spare time visiting Eddie and Jenny on his school holidays. He'd work with his father but what he'd like to do was spend a few weeks staying with them. They had cats and dogs galore; it was a menagerie. Eddie had great practical skills and could do anything with his hands. Ted picked up a lot of skills from Eddie, he seemed to learn something new every time he was there.

At home his father regularly beat them. Any minor indiscretion would constitute a beating with a belt, something his father seemed to take a relish in. His brothers bore the brunt but he saw first-hand what was delivered. His mother turned a blind eye, whether through approval or fear they never knew.

Ted had been supposed to help his father out on one occasion after he'd finished school. Unfortunately for Ted he'd arrived an hour late. His father said nothing but Ted knew he was furious. No explanation was allowed. When he was home he was marched to his bedroom, a leather belt appearing. The beating went on a long time.

His father was a heavy drinker though he rarely drank in company. He had a few select friends whom he visited. These usually turned into heavy drinking sessions. He frequented a lawn bowls club in the summer months. His mother rarely socialised, it was a life of servitude for her, this in contrast to her sisters.

As his brothers got older they both wanted away. The repetition the isolation was getting them down, no future. They listened to the radio when they could. His elder brothers did average at school. The eldest, Keith, wanted to join the Navy but ended up in the Army as did the other, Dougie. Their mother and father gave them no active encouragement to do terribly much. A life of continuation was on offer, what was good enough for them was good enough for you.

The War had changed people's perceptions. People wanted a better life, to enjoy the good things in life, to better themselves, to see their children achieve and have opportunities that they couldn't, to do better. The brothers saw the Army as a way out, to get away, get a different life, training, travel, prospects for now and the future.

Ted being the youngest loved it when his two brothers took him fishing when he was a teenager. Ted had become the latest casualty in his father's fondness for violence. Keith, the eldest, was sick of it. He was leaving in a few months, Dougie would have to wait. Ted had been in all the top grades at school and had become interested in physics, maths and science in general. If they had been of a higher social class Ted would have been bound for another path. The Army though would be his salvation.

By the time Dougie left, Keith had been away for a few years. Dougie was gone, now it was just Ted attending the big school in the local town. He excelled at school. His father was drinking more and the beatings had become more severe. Ted just wanted away. He spent more of his time at his Aunt's. His father was pleased that he was doing well at school, it gave him bragging rights of a sort when he met other men. Ted, although not a natural athlete, was a skilful football player and enjoyed playing in the leagues. Physically he wasn't that big but made up for it in natural ability, it also gave him a chance to get away and meet other lads his age. When it was time to leave school he wanted to join the Army but couldn't get in for another year, so he trained and became a 'French Polisher'. He enjoyed getting away and enjoyed the freedom and money. He spent more time playing football and stayed at his Aunt's more and more.

Keith and Dougie wrote to him every month. They also wrote to their mother and Auntie Jenny. Ted got all the inside information of army life, the good bits, plenty of food, drinking, shooting, women and dances. Ted was mesmerised. It seemed a million miles away. The two were based down in England, Keith had been to Germany for a tour and even to Gibraltar. The stories were great, Ted liked to get an atlas out to see where the two were.

Ted had had word from the Army. He'd been accepted to Signals. He'd be learning electronics and telecommunications. He couldn't wait, he just wanted away. He read umpteen historical books on the war and the Army. He was all set. Keith and Dougie had told him to get into physical shape or he'd struggle.

Ted had problems with his weight: one minute slim the next 'Dougie Bunter'. He could put weight on for fun and not good weight. He did farm labour at the weekends and went hill walking at weekends sometimes helping his father.

His father had got a job with British Rail on top of his other job. The two overlapped, one as gamekeeper for the estate the other for British Rail as Pest Controller. Basically the BR job was catching rabbits; the rabbits were running rife along the rail line. They would set up warrens and boroughs below the rail tracks, this in turn would destabilise the rails causing subsidence and possible disaster such as a derailed train. The pay was better and he got to keep the rabbits. Rabbit stew was a popular dish in the local households during this period. The rabbits were easily captured, setting snares and bag-nets to capture them.

The time flew in. Ted got fit, learned a new trade and his football improved due to his new found fitness. It was off to the Army, no party, no farewell send off, just a goodbye and see you soon. His mother was sad to see him go but showed no emotion, it was the norm.

Ted sailed through his Basic Training, he had passes for leave but never went home. He enjoyed it when the technical stuff started, again excelling and sailing through with flying colours. He enjoyed the combination of outdoors work and blackboard work. He was particularly interested in Telecommunications but enjoyed it all.

The social life suited him, card schools, drinking and along to the dances, he was incredibly shy with women, but the drink helped him along here, it also helped him acquire some sexually transmitted diseases, the phrase put something on the end of it brought a new meaning to them all. Ted was a champion drinker, the nights out were wild, big towns and cities to visit, pubs, clubs, a whole new world, it was the high life all round. Meals and accommodation were thrown in as well.

Ted had made a load of new friends. They were all in the same boat, the majority of them away from home for the first time. It was a mix of the social classes, but they all seemed to get on.

On a particular night out a group decided to go into the local town. They all had twenty-four-hour passes: Charlie, Gregor, Tony, George and Ted. They all had similar backgrounds; working class people, parents all doing similar jobs, fathers as tradesmen, mothers as 'mothers' and housewives. George being the exception, his father a vet his mother a nurse.

They all came from different parts of the country because they were all volunteers and it was a technical regiment so they constantly were taking the piss out of each other. If you weren't Lord Snooty you were a sheep shagger. The regional variations were extreme. Ted did not have a clue what the Geordies were saying, they had no idea what he was on about, a learning curve for all. They were just young lads out for a good time, cigarettes, beer and ready for action. Ted had acquired a car from a friend of a friend who owed a favour. Ted had his licence (just) and designated himself driver (he after all had acquired the said vehicle). They had all had a good few beers before heading off into the local town, all changed into their civilian best. Charlie was the chatty one, he had all that Glaswegian patter.

"C'mon, let's go."

"I'm nearly ready."

"You've had all fuck'n night, for fuck's sake, ya hopeless bastard."

Tony was slapping on some cheap aftershave.

"They'll be after you like flies to…"

"Fuck off!"

"Right are we ready. C'mon, stop arsing around!"

"Ted, is the car ready, driver?"

"Aye."

"Well what we waiting for?"

"George hurry the fuck up."

George had decided to take a case of beer in the car.

"Let's go, let's rock 'n' roll."

They headed off avoiding any figures of authority. Last thing they needed was an evil NCO after them and also remembering to avoid sight of the Mess Hall in particular.

They made it through the main gate, one of the guards on duty was one of their mates.

"Fuck you lot."

"Enjoy your night, hope the Russians parachute in."

Off they went into town, they passed the whisky around. The plan was to dump the car in town and head to a pub then on to a dance hall for afters. Whisky was being passed around like it was going out of fashion. They all had a pocket of cash and were intending on spending it. Ted dumped the car near the town centre in a side street.

"Lock up your daughters, the British Army is in town."

"Shut up, dickhead."

"Fuck you."

The first pub was an old spit and sawdust sort of affair but the beer was cheap and they all got a seat, they had a snooker table as well which they immediately annexed and took over. Ted laughed and drank more, the hand to eye co-ordination of those involved was impaired severely by the fact that they were all half-pissed. They hit the doubles and then hit another pub, this one more upmarket, with doormen on, letting them all pass (first hurdle passed).

"Evening, gentlemen."

They went in and mingled. There were some other lads they knew from the barracks, the boys all on one side the girls on the other – girls predominately seated; just lots of eye contact from one group to the other. They stayed for another. Ted bought a round, his thinking was that it'd be cheaper here than in the dance hall. They were getting restless, truth be told Ted's feet were aching, he could have done with a night on a barstool not at the dances, but that was life.

"Night, lads."

They were under starters orders and off, the establishment in question was at the bottom of the main street down an old cobbled alleyway, out of sight out of mind. It also meant no noise, no complaints and plenty of piss and blood could be distributed on the cobbles along with any other bodily fluids that took your fancy.

Yet another hurdle to negotiate, more of the doormen of the night, this time looking more experienced and hardened.

"Where you been, lads?"

"You here for the night?"

"Busy tonight, lads."

George engaging in small talk with the gorilla bunch, thankfully they all looked like they'd been fed, the boys were in, the place was busy, men up dancing with women, women dancing with other women in groups, men congregating round the bar. Some of Ted's group were in there already, up dancing, no 'Dutch courage' needed here. Ted stood at the bar. Tony had bought a round then disappeared. They all eventually got into the dancing, all up with a girhjl, rock n roll was king.

They lasted the rest of the night, Tony the only one getting past the first obstacle, hauling some local girl into the toilets.

"Romance is not dead."

They all collected themselves to go, the bar had closed, last orders had been called, they were all well-oiled but ready for the road, a quick trip back and into bed. By the time they left they were the last to go, no romance for any of them, Tony though having accomplished the deed. They staggered back up the roads, the place was deserted, singing, singing rubbish, all with a different song all out of tune, all out of their heads, all ready for the short trip home to the barracks.

They piled into the car.

"Right, shut the fuck up!"

Ted drove them, it was a quiet night up an old country road, Ted driving at snail pace, getting nudged at and shouted at to wake up, thankfully a short drive, until disaster. The engine stalled going up a hill.

"Fuck it! Get out. C'mon, I need a push."

"Oh fuck off, will you."

Eventually they got out pushing up the hill, cursing and ranting. A car arrived on the horizon, it pulled over.

"Oh, fuck."

"Evening, lads, anything we can do?"

"No everything fine, officer."

By bad luck a police car on the scene with two boys in blue just our fuck'n luck

"Good night out, lads?"

"Oh yes, officer."

The police knew they were soldiers and heading back to the barracks, they had no interest in prosecuting anyone.

"We'll wait to make sure you get going."

When things looked as if they were sorted Ted accelerated too quickly and took out an old telegraph pole. It was rotten to the core, the car hardly had a scratch, however the telephone line was down and Ted got hauled down the station.

"I think you'll have to accompany us down the station, sir."

"Great."

They all thought this was a great laugh, the group were in hysterics until they were ordered to get their arses back to base by the boys in blue, but not after all their names were taken with proof of id.

Poor old Ted asked to give a sample at the station and couldn't.

"You'll have to wait till the doctor arrives he'll take a blood sample."

The Doctor arrived and the blood was taken, Ted was released in the morning. He was in deep shit, the Army not impressed at this sort of thing. The Army knew before he arrived back what had happened, the police informing them of their boy helping with enquiries. The police gave him a lift back wishing him luck, they knew he'd be punished worse by the Army than anything they could hand out.

A severe punishment from the Army was given, Ted banned from the pub, effectively grounded for three months, any leave cancelled. The rest were told.

"You are all on warnings here!"

"This will be logged in your files!"

Ted also got any dirty manual jobs that were going, if there were no jobs they could be made up, painting stones white a favourite, digging ditches another, pointless and meaningless but the recipient got the jist of the lesson that was delivered.

He attended court a few weeks later and got off with a fine and ban from driving for twelve months and large fine. He also had to pay for the damage.

They had all come into court winding him up beforehand about how he was heading for the 'Big House'. His CO had written a statement about his military service, his aptitude, his model behaviour and how this was extremely out of character blah, blah, blah…

"How do you plead?"

"Guilty as charged, sir."

It was all over in minutes.

To celebrate they took him out on the town and got equally as pissed as the last time, getting themselves into even more trouble this time. This time the MPs lifted the lot of them.

Ted eventually went back home to Scotland. He'd done a lot of training by now and was now based in the north of England, a professional soldier. He'd made it. It'd been well over a year since he'd been back home but he was heading back for a weekend. Keith and Dougie were going to be there; safety in numbers. Keith had left the Army and taken over a pub in the area, Dougie was still in based in the north of Scotland. Both had gotten married in the past year. Ted had attended both but they were stale affairs, the life and soul of the weddings had been the other sides of the family. Ted had been glad to see his Auntie Jenny and Uncle Eddie at the weddings and Auntie Mattie, meeting some of his distant relations always a novelty.

Dougie was staying with their mother and father for the weekend. Ted opted to stay with Jenny, the argument being they had more room, the reality being it was more fun.

The visit got off well, Ted dropped his stuff off at Jenny's, had his dinner. She and Eddie were delighted to see him. He'd come home in his uniform, so handsome, such a handsome young man, all the girls would be after him. He then visited his mother and father. Dougie was there already. His parents had moved into one of the local villages, it was though obvious an incident had occurred. Dougie didn't seem to have unpacked his bags they were sitting in the lobby, his father nowhere to be seen.

Ted made small talk but could feel the tension.

"Nice place in the village."

"Yeh'll be close to the shops."

"Yeh'll have neighbours, what are the neighbours like?"

"Do yeh like it here?"

"There'll be plenty tae dae in the village."

"Wee pub at the bottom of the street."

Fuck this thought Ted, so much for happy families.

"Where's Keith? Thought he was meeting us here?"

Dougie eventually piped up.

"C'mon we'll visit him."

Dougie said bye, left, Ted just said see you later and they were off.

Dougie had a car. Ted noted Dougie was carrying his bags, oh dear, a definite incident then. They both sat in the car no talking, Dougie doing a bit of cursing, a bit of small talk about the two of them, wife fine, army fine

"So what's happened then?"

"Nothing."

"Nothing then, but yir bags are in the car."

"Aye."

"So you're staying with Keith then?"

"Aye."

"Any reason then fir yeh staying with Keith?"

No response

"Where was Dad?"

"Fuck that old cunt!"

Now we were getting somewhere.

"I assume you've fallen out then?"

"Aye, YES!"

"Any reason then?"

"He's a fuck'n old cunt."

That was the extent of the interrogation. It was like pulling teeth, Dougie was saying nothing, nor was his mother. Dougie seemed to be his mother's favourite, his father didn't particularly treat any of them with any favour but he seemed to hate Keith the most. Keith's punishments had gone beyond a beating that left you black and blue. He had ones that had broken bones. They drove the last of the journey in darkness and silence.

They arrived at Keith's pub. Keith had the house that came with it. Dougie got his bags, they went in through the bar door. Keith and his wife, Sheila, were working. Sheila came from Aberdeenshire, she had a weird accent, it took a while to get used to it. She was very dishy, an ideal bar maid; she got the punters in that was for sure.

"WHOA HEY!"

Keith had spotted them then, double whiskies were poured for all.

"So you two okay then?"

"Aye."

"Sheila has volunteered to look after this place, haven't you darling."

"Anything for you, my knight?"

They all laughed, they grabbed a table, Keith just helped himself to drinks, he half worked and half sat with them, Sheila did likewise, all of them drinking and chain smoking, Ted directed a question to Keith.

"Yeh see much of Mum and Dad?"

"Na, well sometimes, you know."

Sheila had answered for him, Keith and Dougie just giving each other a look. Sheila shuffled off picking up glasses heading to the other side of the bar, Ted asked again.

"So will somebody tell me what's happening?"

"Well…"

Keith told all, their father had been on the drink out of control he had beaten their mother badly. She had moved in with Jenny for a while, Ted was thinking Jenny had never mentioned it nor had his mother in her letters to him, Keith was now raving.

"I fuck'n hate him."

Keith was whispering now.

"Ach he's been calling ma Sheila a whore cause she works in the bar, we've never been near their place. He spends his nights in that wee pub in the village. He's a cunt, he's smacking our mother around like it's going out of fashion, but she's fuck'n stupid, just denies it's happening. Jenny's covering up for her."

"He was arguing with me when I arrived, fuck'n moaning about drinking and whoring, I telt him tae fuck off, I'm sick of him, I could fuck'n kill him. Okay if I stay here?"

"Aye."

"Grand."

Oh well Ted thought another great family get together.

"So Ted Gun got yourself a woman."

"What'd you mean one!"

"Ha ha."

The pub had filled and emptied in the time they'd been there, they made small talk, was Keith happy back here.

"Aye hoping to buy a place for myself this place is owned by the brewery, the regional manager comes round every once in a while it's okay."

Dougie and Ted fine in the Army.

Ted was thinking.

"So you going over to see them tomorrow night, I'll need to see them get it over with, I'll stay here tonight, go over to Eddie and Jenny's then skip over."

"Rather you than me."

"I need to see them."

"Okay I'll get yeh over."

Keith had arranged entertainment for tomorrow night.

"Look I've got a young lad that works here as and when, there's a dance tomorrow night in town, Sheila can gae us a lift early we can get a taxi back, some Accordion Band supposed to be no bad, won a lot of rave reviews, wee honey plays the box."

"Accordions."

"Awe fuck off Keith."

"C'mon it'll be hoaching."

"You two are married."

"You ain't."

"Fuck the pair of yis."

The night went on they ended up closing the bar retiring through to the house, Ted had a look round, Sheila said good night told them to behave, they had a few more, Keith went off, Ted and Dougie just crashed out on the chairs and couch, the fire was roaring.

In the morning they had a round of tea, Dougie said he'd drop Ted at Jenny's then come back. Sheila would pick him up in the afternoon at their parents'. They arrived at Jenny's, Ted had a wash and got changed, and Dougie passed the time with Jenny. Eddie was out working somewhere. They all sat for a while making small talk, Jenny gave them tea, sandwiches and cake. The two set off to the parents', Dougie wanting to dump Ted off and head back to the bar.

"Yeh coming in."

"Na."

So Ted was left to deal with it, we'll be back in a few hours.

"Yeh fuck'n better, okay?"

"See ya."

Ted went in, his father nowhere to be seen, Keith racing off down the street like a banshee on fire. Bastard, thought Ted. His mother automatically headed to the kitchen, Ted had a look round, hardly any photos – you'd have thought they had no family.

"Where's Dad?"

"Out."

It then proceeded on to small talk, the Army, did he like it down south, the food; it was just a list of trivia, proceeding on to the lecture, drink, girls, more drink, dodgy people. After two hours of this he was ready to walk out, his father eventually appeared. He was half wasted.

"Just been working up at MacTaggarts."

Ted didn't even know who that was.

"Oh, aye."

Nothing more was said. Fuck this thought Ted, his father asked him a few questions about the Army, more interrogation, blabbing about the new place, he was getting sick of this, wanted away. The noise of a car, thank fuck, Dougie and Keith appeared, a curt hello from everyone, no intimacy, no love lost just a grudging respect or was it resentment, who the fuck knew?

"Yeh okay, Mum?"

"Oh aye."

"Right we're off to town."

"Come across to the pub, Mum, Sheila would like yeh to—"

"Sheila not got a tongue on he?"

Enough of the niceties then, Dougie just walked out, Keith and Ted just said bye.

"Well that went well, I'm still none the fuck'n wiser."

"Get in the car, they know where we are, her in particular. I'm through trying to get through to her. The ball is in her court."

Sheila said nothing.

"C'mon, driver, don't spare the horses."

"Shut it the three of you if you want to get there."

Sheila dropped them off in the town centre putting them on orders to be back at a certain time, we can hit The Cross, nods all round. Ted had never been to any of the pubs in town, this was all new, he'd have a few here just enough to lubricate the wheels, the pubs in the toon seemed okay but not up to the ones he'd been too in the big northern English towns, anyway they'd suffice.

The Dance

The three plodded in to the dance at the Stags Head, paid their fee.

"Go on then get the drinks in."

Ted went to the bar. It was filled with all sorts, not like the northern English clubs he'd been to. They were all filled with the same generation, this was like a zoo, loads of old gits, it was just like a bar with dancing in it. It was lively enough they were half doing Scottish dancing, half just jumping around getting wasted. Drink was flying literally, glasses dropped, glasses spilled, the atmosphere was mental but in an easy-going relaxed manner. However Ted found the music shite, he got the drinks, noted how cheap they were.

"Here you go."

Pints and chasers were the go, they downed the shorts and sipped the pints, Ted looked up at the band, the band-leader was a tiny little dark haired bombshell. Keith was right, she was a looker, a nice piece of fluff. The music was not Ted's cup of tea. Keith and Dougie were just propping up the bar. Dougie got up with some girl and did what was supposed to be dancing, he did not have rhythm that was for sure. More drink was consumed, the band were taking a break.

Ted took a walk outside. It was hot and he was suited and booted. By chance the band had come outside as well through another exit. He said hello, they all responded. Audrey the accordionist smiled at him, her father was there though he looked more like the 'Wild Man of Borneo', you'd be taking your life in your hands.

She came over in the alley, asked Ted for a light.

"Got a light?"

Ted gave her one.

"Thanks."

"Yeh like the music?"

"Aye, it's great."

"Never seen you around."

"Back on leave, staying with my relations, visiting, here with my two brothers."

"Yeh'll have to come and see me without your brothers, I'm playing tomorrow here again. Yeh going to come along, or dae yeh need the heavy mob with yeh... My dad won't be here tomorrow."

"By the way I run the band these days not him. Eight p.m. then don't be late."

179

"Okay."

Ted just nodded, she vanished. Ted went back in wondering if he'd imagined the whole episode, obviously not as she was waving at him from the stage, Keith and Dougie looking.

"Put your tongues back in and lift your jaws of the floor."

"How the fuck?"

"I spoke to her outside that's all."

"That's all, ya bastard."

"I'm seeing her tomorrow."

"We'll have to watch you, yeh cowboy ya."

So Ted was in there, the next day passed quickly, no visits. He got a lift to Jenny's, just went to his room and slept the majority of the day.

Got himself suited and booted, had to tell Jenny he was off.

"Oh are you off seeing someone?"

"Bye."

He arrived back at the venue, it seemed to be empty, no one here no band, just a few locals. Fuck was she just winding him up? Then she appeared. She had none of the Highland Tartan gear on that she'd had on the night before. She waved at him.

He got her a drink. She had a lemonade, he a large whisky.

"Hope you're not a drunkard."

"Oh no, not me."

"Relax I'm joking."

So it was they spent the rest of the weekend together and the romance started. Ted returned back to base and the long distance romance started. Her mother and father giving it the "It'll never last" routine. However, it did. Letters were sent diligently, weekends arranged, even a weekend in the Lake District arranged secretly with a double room, Mr & Mrs G. Ted had gotten all romantic, they'd both come by rail, Audrey lying about where she was heading, Ted telling all his Army buddies he was heading to see his sweetheart.

"Give her one for the lads."

They spent the weekend eating out, Ted had been piling on the pounds (was a Corporal now more money etc), small talk, lovemaking, drinking ensued… the perfect weekend.

Ted let her do the talking. She wouldn't or couldn't shut up anyway so he let her ramble on. They planned for the future, he'd spend more time in the Army get more training, then move back at some stage.

Marriage and bliss were the plan. It never materialised.

7

The Marriage

The Honeymoon

So they were married and a honeymoon to Ireland (Dublin) booked. Perhaps this was the beginning of the end or the end of the beginning depending on how you looked at it.

They went for a week, Audrey stayed with her parents up till the wedding then moved to the flat above the pub.

They went to Dublin via the ferry then rail, getting the ferry to Larne then the train to Dublin. Neither had been to Dublin before, the journey was long, the train seemed to stop everywhere, they felt like they'd seen half of Ireland before they got there. Ted was under extreme instructions not to mention religion nor the fact he was in the British Army. Ted had an unhealthy habit of singing protestant orange songs when one too many had passed his lips.

Unfortunately Audrey didn't know what Ted was like on holiday. Effectively nothing was to his liking – too cold, too warm, food not good, prices…

Ted, of course, had gotten into sarcastic mode, telling Audrey that she'd be bumping into her papist mick relations, he could be related to you etc.

They stayed in a bed and breakfast. There was a Virgin Mary statuette above the bed complete with holy water. Audrey cut her finger and used the holy water to douse her finger in (something she'd come to regret).

They saw all the sites that Dublin had to offer: the streets, the shops, the river, the people. They went to a huge cinema, one of the most modern of its time. They went to see *How the West was Won*.

Another night they decided to go a night to Joseph Locks. He was at the time one of Ireland's premier entertainers and owned a cabaret spot. Ted of course couldn't resist telling them all about Audrey and before she knew it she was up playing someone's accordion. When they found out her maiden name she was treated like the prodigal daughter returning home.

Ted unfortunately took full advantage of the situation. He was knocking into free Guinness and Irish whiskey non-stop. He was soon legless and Audrey had had enough. Thankfully some Irish lads managed to get him into a taxi. Audrey started lecturing, Ted singing, thankfully the driver had a sense of humour and dropped them at the B&B no charge.

Audrey got into bed. Ted couldn't shut up, drink seemed to have this unedifying effect on him, the ability to talk and talk the biggest load of shite. It was also like a broken record, monotonous and repetitive, yapping on about her heritage and roots, just shite.

The next day came, Audrey in agony as her hand had swollen, her cut finger now poisoned, Audrey crying, Ted hung-over needing a drink to smooth things over. Her hand was throbbing, she couldn't stand it, the landlady of the B&B told them how to get to the local hospital. They saw the doctor he lanced the finger, Ted wanting to ask for a drink.

Audrey went back to the B&B. She'd been given drugs. Ted took her back, told her he'd go out for a stroll. Ted's stroll led him to the next street, a little bar and some more of that fine Irish whiskey. Four hours later he went back, Audrey still in bed, Ted drunk, Audrey deciding now she was going home the next day.

The honeymoon period lasted four nights, three days in Dublin, two days travelling. The honeymoon period was certainly over, Audrey yapping all the way back to home. Ted glad when he would get to return to barracks.

They stayed a couple of nights in their new flat above the pub (prime location), Audrey's turn now to moan about things. The noise; at least she got on with Sheila and Keith so that was one good thing. Keith was always the life and soul, Ted took advantage of the situation, free drink for him and his brother the landlord, thankfully the landlady could take control of the pair of them, though Keith could turn on the charm with everyone. Ted returned to base, a rest for him and a rest for everyone else.

Married Life

Ted did his thing and Audrey did hers. She officially stayed above the pub, but spent a lot of her time with her mother and at her brother's. Ted would be away for months at a time, they were strangers in a long distance relationship. Ted's drinking increased. It was Army culture and he threw himself into it. If he

184

wasn't learning new skills he was either on the firing range or in the pub.

He was posted to West Germany for a while. Audrey refused to go, it was obvious she had never given it any thought. Ted on the other hand wasn't rushing back to Scotland, there were bars and fleshpots galore in West Germany. The Cold War was at its height, nuclear weapons, everything had changed, the fear was there that we were minutes away from nuclear oblivion. When Ted had leave he spent his time in one of the German cities, he took in some historical sites but enjoyed the bars and nightlife, he'd never seen anything like it, bands live everywhere. He in effect led the life of a single man.

Audrey on the other hand just looked after her parents, saw her friends, taught music, played and organised the band. This was her routine, she enjoyed it but was jealous of her friends when they were dating, some getting married, her mother telling her she'd been warned, 'you've made your bed you can lie in it blah fuck'n blah'.

When Ted came back he and Audrey were distant. Dougie had left the Army and got a job with a local garage. Ted, when back, spent his time drinking with his brothers. Audrey was always away playing, her life revolved around accordions and music. The constant music was getting on Ted's nerves; if she wasn't practicing she was teaching or on the road.

Their love life was non-existent. Ted had no real interest, when he came back drinking with his brothers, suited his leave time fine. Audrey wanted children, their love making was becoming love less. Ted had more fun in Germany and England than back here, his wife in his opinion was married to an accordion. It wouldn't surprise him if she slept with it when he wasn't there. Give him the girls not the hassle.

Audrey knew she'd have problems having children, she'd had all the problems with her father, but Ted was also seven years her junior. She felt her biological clock was ticking. She felt being with a man, any man, was difficult. She didn't enjoy it, it was mechanical, she loved him but wasn't keen on sex with him or any man. She'd had partners before, but this time it was different, Ted was never rough with her but he had certain expectations and she didn't feel she was meeting them. She tried to satisfy him but her heart wasn't in it and he was becoming disinterested.

After her parents died she felt a bitter loneliness. Her world imploded, she had no real close relatives apart from her brother, she loved him to bits, her aunt she never saw. She didn't like going to her brother's all the time, felt she was imposing.

It was handy that Sheila was there, they were about the same age. Sheila was outgoing and full of fun. She'd met Dougie's wife, the two of them living in the town now. Dougie's wife Jean was outgoing and fun; she was from Glasgow, had all the jokes and sayings and Audrey got on great with the two of them.

Gwen, her new mother in law, had started visiting. Sheila and Jean took nothing to do with her, avoid like the plague they said. Easy for them, it had got to the stage that Dougie and Keith took little to do with their parents.

Sheila announced she was pregnant as did Jean all in quick succession.

"The stork's delivered."

Gwen tried to get involved but the two were reluctant to allow her, she therefore descended on Audrey more and more.

Audrey sometimes took sanctuary during the day in visiting Jenny and Eddie. Jenny was nice and easy going. Audrey sometimes stayed; they were just a lovely couple, couldn't do enough for her, made her relax and at ease. Ted's mother on the other hand had Audrey on edge, everything had to be her way, all the housework hers was the only way, you couldn't get her to see a different point. Audrey sometimes went down to Keith and Sheila's, Sheila taking more time off, so Audrey sat with her, Jean sometimes came across as well. She always livened up the proceedings.

Oz

Ted arrived back. He dropped a bombshell on Audrey. He had looked into emigrating to Australia or New Zealand, he could transfer from British forces to Australian or New Zealand.

Audrey did not respond. It just disintegrated into an argument, her clearing off to her brother's. He, though, didn't want to get involved.

"Look it's up to you two to sort it out. I want fuck all to do with it."

His wife Mary had also just recently declared she was in the family way. Ted decided to move in with Eddie and Jenny for a couple of nights. They were all staying out of it, Keith and Dougie said whatever you think but it's a big move.

Audrey and Ted finally got together. All she did was cry non-stop for a week making herself ill, a transfer was off. Ted told her he'd leave the Army and come back. He'd find something,

187

he wasn't wanting to but he was getting pressured on all sides, changes were afoot.

Babies

So they all gave birth within six months of each other – daughters for Sheila and Jean, a son for Jimmie and Mary. Mary had another son the following year. Gwen was made up. Now Audrey was under pressure, Sheila and Jean her other daughter in-laws had delivered.

"Yir no gettin any younger."

The fact that Ted was never there slipped their minds now. Audrey was lonelier than ever, at least Gwen was off her case. She wrapped herself up in music and started visiting her old friends. It got her out, took more bookings – not always the full band – and she took charity events on her own, anything to get out.

Ted finally arrived back. He'd got money tucked away (as did Audrey). He'd just have to find something. They moved into town, got a deposit on a house, Ted started his own business – an electrical repair shop. He made money but not a lot. They got by but that was it.

In the area there was a Ministry of Defence base. They were looking for Electronic Technicians so Ted was a 'shoe-in'. The business wasn't making enough, Ted spent a lot of time in the pub. It was better, a regular wage and a nine to five to keep him out of the pub. Ted was pleased. All the men he was working with were predominately ex-forces so he fitted in easy.

He had the car so drove out in the morning. He'd regained his licence. His place of work was like that of any military establishment, professional. However there was a bar at the place of work and this was a temptation to all and sundry, if there was a drinking culture there already it was getting a new recruit.

Audrey went at it hammer and tongs for a few years to have a baby, she had a number of miscarriages, this wasn't good with everyone else having children like it was going out of fashion. They were the odd ones out, everyone offering tea and sympathy. Audrey was suffering from depression, trying to put on a brave face, Ted spending as much time away as he could, plenty of sex but very little love. She toyed with tranquilisers. It had become a loveless relationship. Ted always got sad and melancholy when he was drinking. He'd go on binges now for weeks at a time, not bothering with her, storming in at all hours, arguments galore; Ted shouting and singing, record player blaring, hatred on both sides intensifying. It'd become apparent they were not suited, but they'd made their bed so they had to lie in it.

1963

Disaster took place in a few forms in 1963. Keith's wife and daughter died in a car crash. She'd returned to visit her parents in Aberdeenshire. It was a bad road and the time of year meant black ice. Everyone was devastated. Keith, understandably, took it badly. He hit the bottle hard as did his two brothers. Dougie ended up having a heart attack at the start of the year. He had two daughters now. He was only in his early thirties.

Their father John died of a stroke in the summer. Everyone went through the formalities at the funeral but there were few tears shed by anyone, not least the brothers. All their thoughts were still with Sheila. Audrey had announced she was pregnant at the start of the year but that good news had been undone with all the death. A month before Audrey was due to give birth, Dougie died.

The funeral was bad. Everyone was everywhere, everything up in the air. Gwen couldn't go. Dougie had been her favourite. Son, husband, daughter-in-law and grandchild: it wasn't a good year. Audrey looked after Gwen during the funeral. They spent it just looking at the clock; they knew the time of the funeral.

Ted, Keith and Jimmie got hammered. Nothing was said by the women. Keith and Gwen stayed the night. Ted wanted them both out in the morning, running them both back, dumping his mother off, he and Keith hitting the pub, got to give the boy a send-off.

For Keith, father gone, brother gone, wife and daughter gone. A year to forget for all.

1963 and Beyond

Audrey gave birth to a little boy in December. He only lived a week. The doctors made her go to a specialist maternity hospital to give birth. With all her prior medical problems it was deemed prudent. Upon birth the baby was taken to a specialist baby unit. Ted visited, as did Audrey. They named him Keith.

After the death Audrey was bereft with grief. Why her? She wrapped herself up in music but couldn't bring herself to cope with the daily things. It was just another knock back in life. No one said life was easy but this was getting beyond the joke.

Ted hit the bottle hard as did Keith they'd both had enough bad luck, Ted helped in the bar at nights more and more, it gave him an excuse to get out and stay out, Audrey was much the same music taking over, Ted helping on the bar at weekends or shooting and fishing. Separate lives no fun together.

For Ted father gone, brother gone, sister in law and niece gone, son gone, 1963 a year to forget for all.

The Beyond

In the next few years they both polarised their lives. Even Keith was moving on, he'd started seeing another woman, he was starting to go out and socialise, meet new people. He got married quickly he had two sons in quick succession, his life moved on.

Audrey and Ted lived separate lives. Ted had taken to volunteering to go to work at other bases, it kept his pay packet happy. It also got him away. A couple of weeks in Wales or Northern Ireland was looked at with anticipation.

The two never seemed to socialise. When Ted was working at the bar, Audrey never showed face. When Audrey was playing Ted never attended. Her brother, Jimmie, would go along remarking on where Ted was.

"No his sort of thing."

"Mmm."

They both had a life of doing the rounds. Audrey had no interest in any other man. She flirted with the punters – it came with the territory. Ted had an inbuilt shyness when it came to generally dealing with women, some would say people in general. He was happier with animals, acquiring a dog that was usually at his side and keeping it at Jenny's.

As regards children, the two still wanted them, but the heartache that it caused meant it might be a step too far. The marriage was in name only. Jean and Mary visited Audrey a lot with their children, now toddlers, which cheered up Audrey.

But Jean decided to go home to her mother in Glasgow. She'd be sorely missed. Audrey visited Mary a lot whether Jimmie was there or not. The two boys used to come and stay for their holidays as they called it.

Ted spent more time in Wales. The easy life, he thought, military flight up at the start of the week and down fuck'n easy. The MOD had projects going on at one of their major bases in Wales, so asking to be seconded was encouraged, extra pay and expenses and free accommodation came with the package. You could in theory be based there for as long as you wanted. Ted told Audrey he hadn't volunteered but had been ordered, she'd hardly notice his absence he thought and she'd hardly be any the wiser.

Ted had started seeing a woman in Wales. She was a 'Welsh lassie (Florence)' as Ted called her. He liked spending time with her. It was innocent enough. They went to the pub at nights during the week. She stayed in the village next to the base, she wasn't a local.

She worked in the clerical side; he'd met her whilst delivering a form to personnel. She was a bright and bubbly girl, she knew Ted was married, everything was in the open.

Ted ended up in bed with her. After that it was easy, life had taken an upturn, it was noted that Ted was not always staying at the B&B that he was booked into, but no one mentioned it to him. He was becoming closer and closer to her but he didn't know where any of this was going to lead. He was unhappy when home, spending his time working in the bar with Keith, visiting some people, avoiding others (his mother).

He had sex with Audrey, when back, for appearances. It was an emotionless affair. He seemed to drink heavily when back home, the opposite of when in Wales.

Whilst in Wales he spent his time with Flo at her rented flat. She was originally from Swansea. She had got a promotion through the civil service and ended up at the base.

Ted had taken to removing his wedding ring, claiming to Audrey he didn't want to scratch it, also the dangers to his hands when working with moving machinery... It was plausible though half a truth.

8

1967···?

Another announcement at the start of the year – good or bad, time would tell. Audrey announced she was pregnant again. Mary had given birth again, another son.

They'd moved into another house in the toon in Lochryan Street. This would be home for keeps. Ted had left most of it to Audrey. He was on permanent vacation so she'd made most of the arrangements. She'd been spending the majority of her time wrapped up in music.

When she'd announced that she was pregnant perhaps Ted had seemed uncaring and unsympathetic but he'd heard it all before. He was pleased but at the same time filled with dread. Ted didn't want to go through a repeat performance of Keith Jnr, not just the physical aspects but the emotional turmoil. At the moment Ted was happy, he loved being with Flo. In Wales he was anonymous. No one knew him. In Scotland he was Audrey The Band Leader's husband. In Wales he was himself. He loved living there, loved the job, loved being with Flo. Ted though was surprised when she made the announcement, now his mother could get involved.

"It's time you stopped gallivanting all over the place. Get yourself back to your family, you've got responsibilities, a wife a child on the way, roots here."

Keith took little to do with their mother. He had taken over another rural pub; it was far enough away to deter her from arriving unannounced. The only people Ted kept in touch with were his brother and personal friends. He could see the place far enough.

He thought about how he'd been cheated out of Australia, blamed Audrey and his mother. At the moment he was just enjoying life, spending his nights with Flo. The baby situation was a spanner in the works. He'd told Flo he kept nothing from her. She said they'd have to finish if she gave birth successfully. Either way, Ted would lose badly.

Audrey gave birth in August 1967 – a year of footballing highs for Scotland particularly one half of the country. The birth was supposed to have been the 12th or 'The Glorious Twelfth' as it was known, the start of the Grouse Shooting season, but the baby made an earlier appearance. He was named Lee.

It all seemed to be going well. Everyone in Scotland at least was happy. A woman in Wales was broken. Ted made perhaps the biggest regret of his life. Celebrations took place, Lee the centre of attention. Audrey had done it, everyone was ecstatic.

1967–1979

Everyone's life was turned upside down. Audrey cancelled a lot of her engagements though not all. She knew people who could baby-sit for her though it was all chaotic. The noise of accordions did not suit that of a young child. Ted had to make arrangements at work. Half of him wanted to stay with Flo, just tell everyone to Fuck Off! He said his goodbyes to Flo. To say they were both upset was an understatement. When he left he vowed never to return to that base. He kept in touch with letters sent to his workplace in official envelopes. She ended up marrying another man. They both stopped writing.

When Ted returned Audrey thought everything was sorted. Ted though was unhappy with the whole situation. He was happy to be a father, particularly to a son, but was unhappy coming back here. He resented the place. Flo was everything Audrey was not. Flo had been well-educated, intelligent and calm. He could sit all night talking with her about a range of things, politics, sport, work, education.

He had found out the hard way. He'd been with Audrey the best part of a decade but they'd always been apart. This had ticked all his boxes. He got to lead the life of a single man, but he'd had no part in home-building. The relationship was long distance, they had nothing in common. Audrey just yapped at him about nothing – she could talk all night but say nothing he wanted to hear. She would try the patience of a saint.

His mother was visiting more and more. She lived too close for his liking. Australia would have been too close. It was a round of arguments and fallings out with his mother. It was a round of just nodding his head and saying 'aye' with his wife. Audrey spent more of her spare time visiting Jimmie and Mary. She took Lee. Mary had three sons now and was soon to have a daughter, the two eldest now teenagers.

Lee grew up quickly. He took his time to learn to walk, but made his way round the house by crawling, also round Keith's pub as well. Ted went through the motions. He spent a lot of his time at the weekends babysitting, Audrey off with her band. To say Ted resented this would be another understatement, in her words.

"I'm going out to earn a shilling."

"Get a fuck'n normal job like everyone else."

In Ted's eyes she had everything her own way. His drinking escalated. Lee soon started primary school. He'd been fairly happy up until now but over the years the marriage was a sham. Ted found Audrey a pain in the arse. His mother's interference was becoming intolerable.

Hangover and DT Feeling

Ted awoke. It was early morning, well eight a.m. at least. He could hear Lee knocking around, getting ready in the room next door, Audrey up, thank fuck. He'd made it up the stairs at six a.m. He'd finished some Whyte & Mackay whisky before coming up. He couldn't remember where he'd been, ended up in the Railway Club drinking with fuck knows who. Aw fuck he remembered a bit now, he could see a pair of cowboy boots he'd bought in the pub from a Romanian truck driver. Christ some night (or day). I'm coming off the booze though today. He lay in bed half dozing, heard the front door closing. Lee off to school, good lad. Audrey stormed into the room.

"Some bloody state. I hate YOU! I HATE YOU!"

She opened the curtains with the tears running down her face.

"Wasting the day away, remember YOUR mother will be up."

"DRINK. It's the ruination of hames!"

How could he forget? She picked up some washing, screaming at him to give her the clothes he had on and she stormed out of the room. His mother arriving, that would be something to look forward to. She was back up the stairs again, storming about giving him a sore head. Christ, pain in the arse, at least she'd brought him some water.

"Go on stick to drinking that."

"Thanks."

He felt like adding 'Now get tae fuck!'

She opened the curtains to make the neighbours think he was up and not in bed. She stormed off with more clothes. He was thinking about Flo; it took his mind of the crap here.

He got some tablets and swallowed them, a selection from the doctor take your pick, signed off at least from work for two weeks. Doctor had a bad habit of popping in on his rounds though. The doctor was a good sort, used to have a fag with him, but could get ratty. Wonder what Flo would be doing. He thought of her sexually then couldn't be bothered. He was feeling shaky and sick. He needed a drink.

He threw up into a chanty. Fuck this. He tried to stagger to the window, better open it up or the place would stink. He needed a piss but couldn't be arsed going downstairs. His legs were like jelly. He pissed into the chanty, added some Brut 33 to improve the smell. He threw up again, the dreaded dry boke. He lay down for a while. Nine a.m., the front door going, like fuck'n clockwork. His mother.

He heard her yapping away. She'd be up soon to add her piece. The shakes were getting bad and he was sweating like fuck.

He'd need to get a drink. He had a quarter bottle of vodka in his sports jacket pocket. He staggered up and got to it, his head spinning, fell back on to the bed, took a slug or two. He heard the stairs going, hid the bottle beneath the sheets. His mother was suddenly standing there.

"The stink in here. Yir a disgrace."

He said nothing, silence sometimes the best policy. No point in riling a rattlesnake they then tend to strike. She left; he'd got the general gist of what she was saying…nothing he wanted to hear.

Every time he thought about coming off the drink all he got was a fuck'n lecture, yap, yap, yap it was enough to keep you on it, a reality check, why the fuck bother, his nerves were bad enough without this shite.

He heard them farting around downstairs, fuck sake he should give them a hammer to make some more noise, thankfully he didn't need a shite, then he'd have to go down the stairs and confront them to get to the toilet. He finished the vodka. It was ten thirty a.m. He felt a bit better, fuck it she could tidy up. He was puking again, today was not the day tomorrow would suffice for sobriety. He had whisky hidden in the wardrobe, more vodka in the toilet.

He opened a can – he had a couple in the dresser beside the bed. Fuck he hated this. He could hear the postman delivering the letters. He lit another cigarette, it was becoming instinct these days, seemed to be on forty a day Players Navy Cut Unfiltered.

He lay back in bed started to feel more human, slugging on the beer, crushing the empty McEwans Export can. He couldn't stand that lager pish. He opened another can. It was eleven forty-five a.m. – his mother would be going soon. She came round every couple of days to help or interfere depending on your point of view. She just domineered Audrey, Audrey too pathetic to say no. Not like Keith's wives, Jean away back to Glasgow, all the fun reserved for them. Audrey and her farted around with a twin tub washing machine, making a pot of soup too. Fuck'n soup – all his wife could cook. Lee watched a programme called *The Clangers*. They had a character called The Soup Dragon. Ted felt that should be his nickname. They called him TC or Topcat at work after the kids cartoon character. It was his initials, TC, cheeky fuckers. He heard his mother go. Time to get up then he could get tae fuck.

He cleaned up the bedroom and laid out fresh clothes. He only had Y-fronts on, got a clean pair, socks, vest, shirt, tie. He'd hung his suit up, even made the bed, just the empties and puke filled chanty to take care of.

He went downstairs. Great, they had both gone. A note on the table – gone to his mother's then going to shops, soup in pot. He ate some soup, shaved, shit and brushed his teeth. He checked his jacket; wallet, cash, keys. Emptied the chanty into the toilet and cleaned it with bleach then took it back up the stairs. He got his shoes and jacket. He was off, Elvis was leaving the building.

He locked the door and the world was his oyster. He raced off to the nearest watering hole complete with his Elvis Shades. The toon it had won 'Best Kept Public Toilet of the Year' three years on the trot but as TC said,

"Whit do yeh expect from the arsehole of Scotland!"

Audrey had a sense of 'déjà vu'. She'd lived through all this, her mother, her father; at least Ted was never violent towards her or Lee. He made no demands on her, he just seemed to have no feelings for her bad or good. The doctor said he more than likely had a personality disorder but she started wondering if it was her. She started attending church, stopped when she got a letter from the church telling her she wasn't paying enough into the little church envelopes. The cheek of the bastards. She'd once taken Lee to Sunday school. He hated it and refused to go back, so the church days were over.

She tried her best with Ted, but he didn't seem interested in anything she did.

Lee started becoming aware of what was going on when he turned about six. It was non-stop noise. Accordions would be going all day, Ted would be going all night, drinking. Arguments, screaming, shouting, crying, chaos. Audrey would put on a front for everyone. It was happy families, keeping up with 'The Jones'. It became ridiculous.

Ted would sign himself off work for months at a time. He was bothered with back pain from his army days but also heart trouble ran in the family. His place of employment tolerated this because it was part of the culture. Many of his fellow comrades followed the same practice, no one bothered. They would sign off for weeks, even months and meet in the pub. Ted would shuffle off at opening time – eleven a.m. – getting out of the house as quickly as he could.

It was a ritual. Get Lee to school under the pretence of normality. She'd open all of the curtains, Ted usually going to bed when everyone else was getting up. Lee would listen to the screaming and shouting which lasted all night, not really old enough to understand this. Gwen, his granny, arriving up early in the morning, more screaming more shouting. Lee would return from school his father gone, his mother teaching or playing accordions. More noise, more racket, his mother bad tempered shouting at the pupils, bashing the ruler on a table to the beat.

Ted would arrive back between eleven p.m. and one a.m. then the noise and racket would start. The house was a two up two down terraced house. He'd sit at the bottom of the stairs shouting at them both, cooking food, talking to himself, sometimes the record player on. So it went on.

At times Lee became withdrawn at school. He'd gone from Goldstar to Silverstar and seemed lethargic and disinterested. He was bothered with his stomach. He hated one of his primary school teachers who had force fed him, he threw it all back up. He refused to attend for school dinners. He got hit by a car going to school one morning, running straight out in front of it.

He was more and more bothered with his stomach. With nothing physical wrong, a child psychiatrist was called for, the blame squarely lay with the parents, a very unhappy child. According to Audrey it was all down to the accident with the car; someone was in denial.

Lee loved sport, Audrey loved music, Ted was an absentee father. Lee ended up winning loads of sports trophies which pleased Ted but his mother had bought him an accordion. She also had acquired a piano, so learn he did, at least for a while. When at school Lee always had loads of military gear – jackets, trousers, boots. These all acquired from the MoD. Lee always had the latest gear.

Lee liked it when his dad was around and sober. Sometimes Ted would take him fishing. Lee didn't like fly fishing, you could sit all day and catch nothing plus it was always alive with the dreaded midges, Scotland's answer to the mosquito. You ended up being eaten alive, fly fishing was always freshwater fishing beside the burns, rivers and lochs.

Lee liked sea and coarse fishing as you always caught something. Ted took Lee to a spot they'd been before, it was always an adventure. Ted packed all the gear away in the car. It was a little white mini. You could be doing forty miles per hour and you thought you were breaking the sound barrier.

They unpacked the gear. Audrey had made some sandwiches and there was a flask of tea and bottle of lemonade. The bait was not live, just rubber or plastic. Lee loved putting lots of plastic floats on his line, going berserk anytime the float went under the surface. The spot was remote but was only a few miles out of the toon, the coastline just rocks, the sea pounding in. You had to be careful when the tide came up. It was deep, you could be standing on the rocks next to the sea and the depth next to you could be over ten feet. It was like standing next to a swimming pool's deep end. You had the constant wind from the sea, the waves crashing in against the rocks, the noise of sea birds looking for their next meal.

They cast their lines, drank the tea and waited. It wasn't a long wait, this was why Lee preferred it at the sea. Ted caught a couple of mackerel. You never knew what you'd get. Ted claimed to have caught a conger eel in years gone by that was five feet long. Lee had a pull on his line.

"Let it run."

The line went out the fish swimming off, Lee's floats submerged the rod arcing

"Reel it in."

The long haul, it always amazed Lee, the strength of the fish, the pulling power to land it. He reeled the line in slowly, his hands aching, scared he'd let go. Ted was shouting advice at him. He'd caught a dogfish, there was always a tonne of them around; mini-sharks with the teeth to prove it, but tasted like shit so they went back or were used as bait. This one went back to fight another day. Navigating the hook from the fish's mouth was always a small challenge.

Another pastime they both enjoyed was going to see the local fitba team at Stair Park that of Stranraer FC (The Light Blues the only club to pass their centenary without winning a major trophy).

"C'MON, THE FUCK'N BLUES!"

It was always a laugh. There was only one seated stand, the rest was standing room only. Ted liked the standing area. In those days smoking and drinking at the match seemed to be optional. The place seemed to be filled with lots of old codgers and toon nutters wrapped up in coats, scarves and hats screaming constant abuse at the referee and opposition players.

Ted always made sure they both had either Bovril or Tea and a scotch pie (the tea was always like piss and the pies oh the pies). The result was irrelevant which was just as well as Stranraer were not the Liverpool of the north, but there was entertainment to be had. In Lee's eyes there were not enough days like these. These were childhood memories to remember.

Another favourite occasion they had was going to the cinema. The trouble was the cinema was thirty miles away in another small town. They always went to the latest James Bond movie. Lee remembered going to see 'The Spy Who Loved Me' with Roger Moore.

"He's nae Sean Connery that Moore."

A child at the cinema kept shouting at the screen for the first half of the show.

"Where's Jaws? Where's Jaws?"

Ted had had enough of the yap

"Look, son, shut the fuck up will yeh?"

Diplomacy in action?

Holidays were always fun for Lee. He just hung out with his mates, football and bike rides the order of the day.

Ted and Audrey decided to take Lee on holiday. The farce had started. Remember holidays were, supposed to be, fun. The holiday, if that's what you want to call it, was to be for a week at a local caravan site. They were to stay in a four-berth caravan, owned by Audrey's brother, Jimmie. A fuck'n disaster couldn't have been better planned it was the holiday equivalent of 'Operation Market Garden'... GREEN ON GO!

The caravan site was a few miles outside of the toon. There would be no problems with jet lag then. Audrey took the car and drove. The reason she was driving was because Ted was on holiday too and had been on the drink since he clocked-off his work, and that was Ted's idea of entertainment.

On arrival it was okay. At least, it wasn't raining. The caravan was fine, Lee disappeared to the beach, Ted just disappeared.

Ted headed off to the caravan site bar. He knew the owner of the site so proceeded to get stuck in, it was open all day.

He then navigated himself over a couple of fields to get away. It was now 'The Great Escape'. The problem for all and sundry was that at Ted's workplace they had a works bar fully-licensed with club prices. The fact that Ted technically could have been shot by climbing the fence onto MoD land didn't seem to bother him. He knew all the MoD Police any way, hopefully they'd recognise him and not shoot.

Lee made a couple of friends on the beach. They had a football so 'fitba' was the order of the day with shirts used as goalposts, no need to worry about sunburn – you needed the sun for that.

Lee returned to the caravan. Audrey had brought a load of sandwiches for the first night. There was nothing to do at night, no television, no nothing. Ted was missing but you didn't need many guesses as to where he was. Audrey and Lee amused themselves for the night. Audrey read some magazines, Lee had brought a Lego kit and built a tractor before heading off to one of the bunks for bed.

They both got themselves ready and went off to bed. The inevitable happened of course. Ted came back making a racket, more than likely waking up half the caravan site, trying to find the correct caravan. At least the other holidaymakers had come some considerable distance to the place, not six miles. Ted found the caravan, nearly breaking the door coming in

"Hello, are yeh awake?"

"HELLO, ARE YOU AWAKE?"

Well if we weren't awake then we are now. Ted proceeded to rustle around, falling around, wanting something to eat, just jumping on one of the berths talking, shouting and singing all night. This was interspersed with Audrey telling him to shut up, be quiet. This went on all night. This lasted only another night. The holiday was ended by mutual consent, Ted returned to resume his activities in the toon.

Ted's health took a turn for the worse. His back was in agony. He'd slipped discs in his back he was put into traction, and moved to a specialist in Glasgow. He was in hospital for months. It gave everyone a rest. Lee had a load of friends at school. He'd joined a lot of clubs and spent the majority of his time in the local woods or beach and kicking a ball around the park. They could also go bike rides in the countryside.

There were always arguments about money. Everything was in Ted's name regarding the bank accounts and bills, so when he was admitted to hospital this of course caused problems. Audrey could never understand any of it though Ted did try to explain it to her stating.

"Yir too fuck'n stupid."

Audrey then technically a housewife, Ted stating she should learn to cook a decent meal if that was going to be her forte. One time she'd been cooking in the kitchen, Ted and Lee watching the television in the living room. She'd run into the living room, her hair all burned. She'd had a grill that had caught on fire. She'd ran out the back door with it and then the wind had blown the flames on to her, singeing all her hair and burning her eyebrows off. On seeing her running into the living room Ted had burst out laughing and said,

"Frying tonight?"

This was a reference to the film 'Carry on Screaming' which had viewed the night before. Both he and Lee had gone into fits of laughter.

"Yir nothing but pigs."

No dinner tonight then.

Audrey and Lee visited Ted in hospital every once in a while and they both wrote. Audrey had her brother visiting and vice versa. Lee got on fine with his cousins. Jimmie had a son a year older than Lee and a daughter a few years younger. The two boys got on great, Lee liked visiting them in the village, the countryside was on tap. That was his summer holidays.

Pets and animals were always there in the household; a dog, a large cat and a tortoise. The dog was named lassie, the cat tiger and the tortoise had no name. It should have been called Indestructible as it still lives to this day. Lee had a fondness for the cat and he crept into Lee's bedroom in the middle of the night on numerous occasions.

Ted eventually returned to work. He hated the place. He was an unhappy man. He'd never hit Lee before in his life. Then Lee had wound him up. He wasn't even on the bottle or hungover. He hit Lee. Ted was mortified, couldn't believe he'd hit Lee. Lee was slightly in shock as it had never happened before.

Lee got marched down to the local sports shop. Lee could spend all day in these places. He loved the times they went on a day shopping trip up the coast to Ayr. They had BIG sports shops in Ayr.

Ted was on a guilt trip. He knew he wasn't the best father and husband but he had never hit either Lee or Audrey. Lee was kitted out with the full Scotland strip

"Boots would be nice."

"Dinnae push it."

"A new mitre ball too."

"Shut it."

Both were purchased.

The years went by. Ted was admitted for alcoholism and sent off to rehab. Lee was to start secondary school. Audrey had become manic, screaming, shouting, violent, constantly talking, yapping, everything that went wrong was someone else's fault. She hated being wrong. She was always right, ALWAYS.

Ted's drinking was squarely out of control. He was never off it. The amount he was drinking was astronomical. There were occasions he was admitted to hospital, they effectively just dried him out and put him on his way.

Things reached a head when he started hallucinating. The police were called, scared he was armed and dangerous, a shrink was called for. He was off to a specialist unit, Audrey telling everyone it was his back again, no one quite believing her, this time he was off to a secure unit.

He was admitted there for a while; detox and counselling, effective rehab, no visitors. Ted was glad to get away but whether any of this helped was debatable. Ted even told them.

"The horse bolted a long time ago, bit late fir shutting the fuck'n gate eh!"

At least it gave everyone a rest. The psychiatrist had said that Ted's drinking was due to personal trauma and the fact he hated his life, in particular his wife and mother.

"Tell me something I don't fuck'n know."

The women of course responded in their usual manner, Ted responded in his.

"Sober up, square yourself up."

Response:

"Fuck off ya witches!"

So the fun went on. Audrey led her life, music, and Ted went on with his. Lee started to dislike the pair of them. They were completely wrapped up in their own worlds. Audrey spent her time doing the usual (music) and Ted had taken up bowls and golf. It got him out the place.

Over the years Ted's uncle and aunt, Eddie and Jenny, died. Eddie keeled over in his nineties. He'd had a good innings, died in his beloved garden. Jenny went to a home. She only lasted a few years after Eddie's death.

By the end of the seventies Audrey's band had seen its day, some of the members moving away, moving on, moving to another world. Audrey took to playing with a fiddler with the name of Rory. He was a prodigious drinker, eventually to his ruin, his liver would vouch for that.

Audrey kept on playing without the band. Rory was a fine musician but he did have the problem with the bottle, breaking many violins in the process much to his financial cost. The toon had quite a crowd and a large bunch of amateur musicians. Audrey's style of music however was in the descendency, rock and pop were king, the old style would survive but its heyday and popularity had gone.

9
Jimmie (Brether)

Jimmie had always been a part of Audrey's life. Everyone remarked they were more like twins than brother and sister. Over the years they were always there for each other. Audrey always had her music but Jimmie played a big part in a lot of this. He founded a local Accordion Club. It met once a month and drew big crowds in the seventies. Jimmie got on fine with Ted but they were never close. They both moved in separate circles, Jimmie and Mary living in the village, Ted and Audrey in the toon.

They visited occasionally, always at New Year, Ted never keen on going to see Audrey play, always an excuse for him to do his own thing. Jimmie would turn up, do his MC routine and sing a few songs, always getting a laugh and telling a few jokes, copious amounts of drink always consumed.

"I love yeh, brether."

"I love yeh, sis."

Jimmie had taken over from where his father had finished. The horse trade had declined over the years, agriculture going mechanical. Thankfully though 'The Hunt' remained and show jumping had taken off. The gentry and general snobs felt it necessary to own an equine animal to seal their status, or something like that.

Jimmie and Mary had four children, three boys one girl. Only one would follow the family tradition. Jimmie, like his father, was hard to please and a hard task master, the first two escaping the grind. The last one eventually did not.

They had lived in a few houses over the years in the village. They never moved into town and were happy enough, there were a few shops still going, the baker's long gone.

Jimmie had found he could get a load of work doing 'non horse' jobs but loved working with them, he was all for tradition. Like his father he had ruled with an iron rod, his fists too familiar with the rest of the family. Drink was also a familiar part of his diet. He did have his father's Jekyll and Hyde relationship with drink, though to the outsider he was the life and soul and a natural comedian.

In the village he had been nicknamed 'The Moth'. This was because of his habit of, when returning from a night out, if he saw a light on in any of the villagers' houses he'd make a beeline towards it, demanding a drink and party. Long nights often ensued.

His antics were famous and infamous. He did have a great deal of get up and go and an endless supply of energy. He liked a drink, a story, and a singsong. He'd become quite a local celebrity and seemed to be constantly socialising, even taking an active interest in politics (Scottish Nationalism), unlike Ted who thought all politicians were,

"Fuck'n arseholes."

So Jimmie was Mr Scotland through and through.

"There'll always be an England as long as Scotland stands."

One of his long time commitments was setting up the 'Accordion Club' in the local area. He could never play but he tried learning the 'button-box' and could play a little by ear.

In the seventies he made a bold move. A group of blacksmiths from Scotland decided they'd attend the Blacksmithing World Championships in Canada. It was an 'American Rodeo' style event in Toronto so they entered a team and won. They all knew each other having competed against one another at various Agricultural Shows. On the trip there they flew from Prestwick to Canada. Jimmie was carried onto the aeroplane, a good time was had by all, Scotland the winners.

Of the group the majority had never been up in a plane, so they all made the local and national news and had their moment of fame. Jimmie had a great time and was asked back a few years later. He'd made so many new contacts. The next thing he knew he'd been invited to a Canadian college, talking about metal and the trade in general.

A few years later he had a visitor from the USA, a rodeo champion he'd met at the competition in Canada. Ray was a rodeo champ. He owned a ranch in Arizona but made a load of money entering these competitions. He was allegedly half-Cherokee.

He stayed a week, all the locals nicknamed him 'Marlboro Man'. He certainly didn't disappoint. He was an one hundred percent cowboy, the real deal. Jimmie took him out to a Pony Riding School, he had a job on, shoeing some horses. They met the woman who ran the place. It was all a bit 'la-di-da', the landed gentry. Ray asked,

"Mind if have a ride on one of your ponies?"

There was a selection in the adjoining field.

"I'll get one saddled up for you."

"No need, mam."

Ray took a running jump at one of the ponies. He vaulted on to the back of the animal, riding the horse round the field, navigating umpteen jumps. He did all this bareback. Jimmie couldn't stop laughing. The owner stated,

"Oh my!"

A legend was born, the spaghetti westerns had come a calling.

Jimmie had a regular customer, Frazer, who ran a team of Clydesdale horses as a hobby, but they paid their keep, making appearances at events. He also used Jimmie as his blacksmith. The pair had their fair share of nights out. Frazer had been asked to provide his team for Tennents Brewery. They'd pull an old fashioned beer tanker. The event was the St Patrick's Day Parade in Dublin. There was only one answer; Frazer, of course, would need his trusty blacksmith.

On the parade the pair sat up the front, Jimmie's job was to hand out beer cans to the revellers in the crowd. A good few cans, and whiskey, however were consumed before, during and after the Parade. Jimmie fell off the wagon in one of Dublin's main streets and after an extremely heavy night woke up with the horses (no form of animal cruelty took place).

The trip there and back was eventful. They were delayed in Northern Ireland due to bad weather (no ferry), so another night was had by all in Ireland. Hangovers were complete. They had made such an impression that the brewery hired them for other events. It was a tough job but somebody had to do it, remarked Jimmie.

When Lee moved away he always gave Jimmie a visit when he came back, usually with a girlfriend. Jimmie always making some sexist remark. Lee knew there would be an ample supply of drink, but when he'd been abroad on holiday he always brought him a supply of duty-frees, consisting of cigarettes and whisky.

His violent temper never left him. On one occasion he'd had his anvil stolen from his smithy, something that didn't amuse him. He knew it was a local, either for spite or a laugh. He wasn't laughing. He'd been at one of the other villager's houses on Hogmanay 'first-footin'. He went for a piss outside to find his anvil hidden away in the garden. A punch-up ensued and a severe kicking – justice was served.

The cunt had his coupon kicked.

He'd been on another wild night returning to find the door to the house locked. Unable to find his keys in his mood (Mr Hyde) this would not do. He couldn't get in. Instead of knocking to get in he went round the back of the house. Not bothering to try the back door, he acquired a sledgehammer from the shed and returned round to the front door. In his state he kept missing the door and hitting the wall holding up the door, eventually taking out the door and a large part of the side wall.

He had a local friend Davie who he used to go drinking with. They ended up with a group of other locals in a neighbour's garden on a summer's day. Davie got well and truly hammered. He was only allowed out by the wife for a specific period of time.

There were a couple of stone steps to navigate from the garden to the main house. Davie was worse for wear and tripped, rendering himself unconscious. A 999 call was required. Jimmie insisted on going with him and jumped into the back of the ambulance. Davie was on the stretcher getting his eyes examined upon which one fell out. It was fortunately glass, but it was enough to revive the patient and cause him to dive out the back door of the moving ambulance. So much for concussion.

Nights and days like the latter were common place. Whisky – or whatever took the fancy – was an integral part of socialising and the goings on of the village. Parties took place on a whim. No one was a millionaire but there was a community spirit – spirit perhaps the best word for a lot of the goings on. No one felt alone and there was a common bond.

Jimmie could, however, take things to excess. He had extremely conservative, old-fashioned views on a lot of areas, a wife should know her place being in the top list.

He'd been out for the day. It could have been any day, he'd been at a local fair in the toon. *'Only here for the beer'* was the cry. By this time the family had grown up and moved out, just him and Mary. Jimmie had his moans and gripes about all his children but got on well with all of them particularly in his latter years. Perhaps he'd mellowed. He liked the fact he had grandchildren and spoiled them rotten. He was Granddad Jimmie, everyone liked to remind him. Secretly he liked to be reminded.

The beer and chasers had flowed. He'd fallen in with a group of farmers and farm workers so the drinking was robust, besides it was a nice summer day – to be nice all it needed was NO RAIN.

The fair consisted of a number of things: rides for kids, hot dog stands, events such as dog-handling, horse jumping, baking competitions, assault courses, but the bread and butter of the event was the judging. This consisted mainly of agricultural animals such as cattle and sheep but there had in recent years been the more 'exotic' such as limas, the smell of shite wafted in the air.

After this they filtered away. Jimmie descended on a local pub, songs were sung, jokes told, old stories told and re-told, glasses raised to absent and attendant friends.

The ring of the bell and the cry descending too soon.

"LAST ORDERS!"

Always a time when the hardened drinker would race to the bar as if their life depended on it, buying in a couple of pints or doubles usually with umpteen drinks waiting to be consumed at the table long forgotten about, referred to by bar staff as wastage. Jimmie went to relieve himself, his bladder suffering due to age and quantity of liquid as much as anything else. He staggered back, said his good nights to all and sundry. He'd cadged a lift off someone back to the village, dropped at the doorstep, a result of a day; free taxi service home

"Cheers for the lift, see ya."

Light on, Mary still up. She could get him some food. He staggered in she looked at him.

"Look at the state of yeh, for Christ's sake get to bed."

"Dinnae be telling me, get me something to eat."

"Get it yirself."

This was not the answer that was expected or wanted. Jimmie slapped her hard then went into a rage, hitting her face. He then completely lost control, wrapping his hands round her neck. He was literally foaming at the mouth, screaming abuse, his head throbbing, the adrenalin pumping. He squeezed her neck tighter and tighter. Something had to give. Jimmie's face looked ready to explode; his eyes looked as if they were about to pop out of his skull. Co-incidentally, Mary looked identical. Jimmie let go, his chest heaving.

"Whit the fuck yeh daein! Tryin tae gie me a heartache! Ya cunt."

Mary gasped for breath. Jimmie staggered to the kitchen and took a bottle of whisky from the cupboard below the sink. He wandered into the garden and sat on a deck chair. This was where he woke up some time later.

When he returned to the house Mary had cleared out. He lay on the couch still drunk. He awoke again to find a couple of police standing over him. He was hauled in questioned, released and warned.

Mary had gone to one of her sons. He had phoned the police. She moved in with her son for a good few months, no apology ever forthcoming. Things were testy for a good few months but she eventually moved back in.

Audrey, of course, took his side, knowing he'd done wrong and also knowing that this wasn't the first time this had occurred.

"I knaw he's done wrang bit he's ma brither."

When all this happened his family ostracised him for a spell. He never said sorry. It was his nature and he couldn't change it, it was like the old story of the scorpion and the frog.

The scorpion and frog had a chance meeting at the side of the river. The scorpion wanted to get to the other side.

"Let me ride on your back so I can get to the other side."

"No, you'll sting me."

"Why would I do that? I'd drown."

"What's in it for me."

"I'll be your friend."

The frog thought about the advantages of this offer.

"Okay."

In the middle of the river the scorpion started stinging the frog.

"What are you doing? We'll both die."

"I'm afraid it's in my nature."

Jimmie did know he'd done wrong.

He died a few years before Audrey. He died of problems with renal cancer. Cigarettes, alcohol and manual labour would also be contributing factors. He couldn't complain he'd had a good run in for the life he led.

10
1979···?

Lee had started secondary school. This was a new challenge; no longer a child, though there were times when he wondered who the child in the set-up at home was. In secondary school the work became more challenging. More clubs were on offer, more sports clubs to join.

Everyone in the household led their own lives so Lee followed the trend. By the early eighties Ted's drinking was out of control. He was in hospital constantly, bouts of heavy drinking. Audrey led her musical life religiously, teaching, practicing and playing. Problems of money always reared their head when Ted was away. Everything was in his name. Audrey's argument for playing was 'to earn a shilling'. Ted always told her to get a real fuck'n job like everyone else.

In the early eighties Keith, Ted's brother, had a car crash, breaking both his legs. It brought back bad memories of his first wife. He was laid up at the pub for a long time. Ted would disappear and visit him. Drinking, of course, was part and parcel of the visit, the two getting drunk, Keith shuttling around on crutches. Keith put on a lot of weight after the crash; he was not as active, indulging in heavy drinking, heavy smoking and living in a pub. He died of a heart attack. Ted buried his brother, his mother unable to attend due to grief. Lee spent the day of the funeral with her. She visited the home of Ted and Audrey even more. Ted was never there.

Ted returned to work after one of his drinking bouts. His work was all very hush-hush, basically testing the latest high-tech gadgets the MoD had to play with, laser guided missiles and such. Ted had been doing some testing on the shoreline when he keeled over. He was in his mid-forties and had had a massive heart attack.

It was touch and go for a while. He spent a while in hospital, probably one of the few times he was admitted when sober. On his discharge he returned home, signed off for a while, returning to work but ending up back in hospital.

A bypass was called for, a major operation if ever, back to Glasgow. At least he got to see Jean. She'd remarried, had another couple of children. She still the same as ever, larger than life. She was a tonic.

A few years earlier Ted, Audrey and Lee had attended the wedding of Dougie and Jean's daughter. It was a drunken affair and it brought back memories, not all of which were pleasant. The wedding was in church and reception was held in an Orange Lodge. The month prior to the wedding the Lodge had been raided by the Police who found a load of dynamite hidden. The wedding celebrations lasted a couple of days, a load of alcohol consumed, life goes on.

The operation was in the Western General, Glasgow. Ted hated hospitals. His time with back problems had made sure of that. The bypass was complex but they had the best doctors in the world for this operation. The surgeons had the potential for more practice than anywhere; Glasgow was 'Heart Attack City'.

After the operation he returned home and recuperated for a while. He was weak and shaky. Forced to give up drinking and smoking before the operation, his mood was not good. He returned to work after a spell but was retired on ill health. He wasn't even fifty yet. He just wasn't suited for the manual side of the job and with no desk job on offer. It suited Ted fine. He got a MoD pension, Army Pension and State benefits. He'd paid in so time to get it back. He then seemed to make a miraculous recovery.

He was then never home, constantly away in the pub, playing bowls, fishing. He lived the good life. He was plagued though, with the drink which lead to him having more heart trouble. He had constant spells in hospital, in and out. The relationship between himself and Audrey was non-existent. He couldn't be arsed with her, blanking her sometimes when she visited.

For Lee it was pretty much life as usual. He'd visit Ted in hospital; he got on fine with his dad when he was sober, but found him a pain in the arse when not. As regards his mother, their relationship blew hot and cold, becoming more polar as the years went by. Lee had started playing squash and become a good club player, competing at a high school level, also playing football in the summer leagues and running in the school athletics team.

Ted found himself out bowling more and more. He'd run in with a good social crowd. If they weren't bowling they were drinking to the early hours. At the bowling club Ted had a key and was on the committee. In summer months he sometimes stayed the night at the club, in the cellar. The cat had roosted with the pigeons, peace and quiet for everyone.

Audrey would go to the bowling club if Ted had been missing too long telling him to return home. The response was predictable 'something off'.

Ted had never been close to Keith's sons but was devastated when one died in a motorcycle accident. He was now burying his nephew, his mother now losing another grandchild. For a while Keith's was hitting the bottle, though who could blame her.

Ted's mother now lived in a little flat but life had taken its toll. Ted avoided her. The only person who visited was Audrey, sometimes Lee, though Lee tired of her constant questioning about her son, his father.

"Is he drinking?"

"No."

It was the favourite question.

When Lee attended the doctor he was asked a similar question.

"Ted being a good boy?"

"Yes, doctor"

"You'd bloody say that anyway." The doctor would say this with a smile.

Lee was lucky in that he ran around with a good crowd. All did well at school and in future years went on to do great things. They liked to socialise together and hang out like teenage kids do, listening to records, going to local discos.

Lee loved playing squash. It was here he realised that he really had to do things for himself; he decided he was going to enter a national squash competition.

He had some money set aside and went off to do it. The competition was in Edinburgh, not next door to the toon, so it took a bit of planning. It was his first time in the capital city. Lee got tickets arranged. Early train Saturday seven a.m., got up there at ten a.m., competition started eleven a.m. Lee was a wild card entry – not seeded. His first match was against the second seed, beat the bastard 3–1. At the end of first day he got to the quarterfinals, lots of questions about who he was, the Irishman, 'I'm not Irish'.

The trouble for Lee was that the quarter-finals were the next day, Sunday. He had some money and went to bar then left the venue, walked around all night, tried to sleep in a park. Luckily it was June. The quarterfinals happened, Lee hadn't much energy but was only beaten 3–2 (the cunt) Unlikely he'd want to play for any national team anyway too far to travel. Fuck it.

The comparison for Lee was an eye-opener; everyone fairly posh all there with their families, driving up in Volvo estate cars, he arriving alone on the bus. No support, no help, on your own boy! When he arrived back he told no one. It was enough that he knew.

Unemployed

When Lee left school he hadn't planned anything. Everyone he hung around with knew what they were doing or planning to do or at least their parents did. Lee on the other hand had just been going on as usual, no ambition, minimum at school, sport, socialising. School ended, now it was choice time.

He was too late to apply for college, he hadn't even tried. All he wanted was to get away, everyone he knew left to go to university or college, a few stayed to join family businesses, some joined the armed forces.

Getting a job in the toon if you knew no one was impossible. Ted no longer worked there, there were no family contacts. Ted, when working, had got one of Jimmie's sons an apprenticeship with the MoD. This no longer an option.

For Lee this was a long year. He went to night school and got some more qualifications. It passed the time. He started applying for every crap job going, no luck. Dole money was crap. He applied for college, police, army. The result was accepted for Army but a one-year waiting list (too long), accepted for the Police Cadets Metropolitan (couldn't see himself living in London. Never been South of Carlisle), accepted for college (drink and women). A foregone conclusion then, the great escape was on.

Ted decided one day to hit the pub. It was one of those all day affairs he so much loved. He'd gone to a local bar, ran in with some of his drinking buddies. Doubles were being downed at a horrendous rate and that was the story of the day. A few days went by and Ted was labelled 'Missing in Action'. Audrey had not seen hide nor hair of him until a phone call was received. In Spanish.

"Ola?"

Eventually Ted came on the phone. The story was that on going to the bar he'd ended up on a coach to see some football match. The trouble was the match was in Spain, further trouble was that they all thought it'd be funny not to tell him when they were leaving back to the UK after the match. So he was stuck in Spain with no passport or ID and with the money running out. How he got back was one of life's little mysteries, he had the survivor gene, that was a given. College time.

1986–1998

Lee packed his bags, it was time for mayhem of college. One of his cousins (Jimmie's son) had agreed to drive the car, Ted on the drink, Audrey yapping.

"I don't know why yeh cannae get a job local."

"There are fuck'n none, remember."

"Yeh'll be getting up to no good."

"Hopefully."

"Remember to phone and write."

"I'm not there yet."

So the agenda was set for a four-hour car journey, the insistence of a bar lunch before unpacking a must. It was a chance for Ted to refuel and Audrey to gain wind for more moaning on the return leg.

Lee had memories of the time he had gone to the squash tournament. Everyone else would be there with 'normal' parents encouraging them, helping them and what the fuck had he got? A fuck'n walking circus, an embarrassment in progress, the loony tunes. Lee picked up his keys, went through the administrative formalities. They then unpacked his stuff into his room in the Halls of Residence. Thankfully there was no one around, minimum embarrassment.

Ted stuffed a wad of notes into Lee's pocket.

"Thanks, Dad."

"Don't do anything I wouldn't."

"Licence to do anything then, 007."

"AAAgggghhh!"

Ted now tapping his nose, Lee half expecting a packet of Durex to be given to him. Audrey now wanted Ted back in the car, and off they departed, thank fuck. He went to his room, unpacked his stuff, posters up, looked at the normal people from the windows. The parents were crying when they left their children, would have been nice.

For Lee the years at college went by quickly. He reckoned they were some of the best in his life. Reality was always there when he returned home. Audrey had cut back on her pupils, her engagements to play were rarer. She had an operation on one of her hands. It was repetitive strain, tendons had to be sorted.

Ted did his usual. The bypass had given him a new lease of life so Ted was 'bowled' away and drinking like it was going out of fashion. He had been cured. Hallelujah!

When Lee graduated he didn't go to the ceremony. On asking Audrey if she wanted to go he got her usual response.

"Would they no be better of gettin yeh a job, eh!"

That was it, Lee thought. I wonder what the reaction would have been if it had been an accordion tournament. The tribe would have descended upon the capital city.

After college he and one of his friends headed to Israel working on a Moshav, in a Kibbutz. You're a volunteer in a Moshav, a paid volunteer.

Mother's reaction was predictable.

"Yeh'll be killed."

Father's reaction: "Get fuck'n in there!"

Lee eventually settled in Edinburgh. He had various jobs, added to his qualifications at night school, on gaining a BA his mother's reaction was, "Mmmhhh."

On gaining an MSc.

"That'll be you then, you'll think you are something."

It would have been nice if his mother had thought that, at least his father said he was pleased. Lee's visits to the toon declined. He had several relationships over the years, went back home occasionally. He came to dread it though, dealing with the parents. The new women in his life didn't mind visiting the toon, all a bit quaint, the history and past immune to them.

1996

Lee took various jobs, landed a project in Africa which he enjoyed. It was an experience. On arriving back he went away a weekend to London. On coming back a message left on the answer machine from one of his cousins to phone home. He knew what the message would be, question was which one.

His father had drawn the short straw then. The relations were desperate for Lee to return home, only to deal with the wailing Audrey. Who could blame them? Not the most pleasant of jobs.

Ted had been badly ill for six months, Audrey accusing him of being with another woman, the relations just agreeing with her anything to shut her up. One of Lee's cousins phoned him to tell him this startling revelation. Lee didn't believe a word of it. His father was many things but not that. Physically it was beyond him anyway.

Ted had been away all day at a bowling tournament. At the time he was heavily on the drink; non-stop boozing was the order of the day. Home life was rubbish so his time was spent bowling or drinking. He enjoyed the social life the patter, the drinking.

It was 'The Glorious Twelfth of July' so it was party time in a lot of parts of Scotland, Orange parades up and down the country. Ted had gone off to a bowling tournament in Glasgow, a couple of drivers designated, entry to the competition a formality. They would watch a March whilst there, and then return back to the toon. The result of the tournament was irrelevant. Drink was consumed by all involved. Ted went a pub-crawl on their return. He fell asleep in the living room on a reclining chair. Audrey never heard him returning home, he never made a sound and he never woke again. Cardiac Arrest, sweet dreams….

Funeral

I arrived back the next day, the funeral set for the day after. At least they'd managed that, relations disappearing as soon as I arrived. Time for the tirade. *Where were you? You don't care.* So it went on. My mother now had someone new to yap at. I knew from the point of my father dying I'd inherited the baton. It had been passed. My mother just yapped

I went out with my partner of the time, got some food in, got some booze in. The booze was essential. The next day went quick. I packed my mother off to bed to try and get some peace, the doctor had come round gave us a prescription for pills. A good excuse to go out and have a drink. I ended up getting drunk the night before, ended up getting half-drunk before the funeral and after it, thank fuck I had the excuse of work to go back to. No after funeral drink, just the usual pish. My Uncle Jimmie up for it but that was about it (he was always up for a drink). Got away after sorting out some things for my mother, things I'd be inevitably be to blame for in the future. The lightning rod had been passed on.

I never really thought of my father's death in any way, apart from how to deal with my mother. It was to be a long haul.

11. 1998–Now

I split with my partner of the time in 1997 – it had been a turbulent year for me – and moved to London. I got married and divorced had a son and enjoyed it all but it unfortunately came to an end. After London I worked all over the world and then came back by chance – destiny or fate, if you believe in that sort of thing – to the toon. All I can say about my relationship with my parents and particularly my mother was.

"I tried."

"Let the merry-go-round resume."

The End (for now)